PERMANENT
MOMENTS

Permanent Moments

A Fictional Autobiography

Illustrated by the Author

Stephen Mitchell

To order additional copies of this book, contact:
Xlibris LLC
1-800-455-039
www.Xlibris.com.au
Orders@Xlibris.com.au
514038

for my wife

Jackie Owen

and our children

Jessica

Oliver

and

William

No matter how miserable I may be
you can always be depended on to make me laugh.

DEAR READER

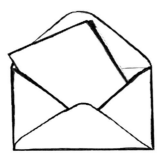

I'll bet you're wondering why this book is called *Permanent Moments*.

Well then, let me explain:

Back in 1979 I read a review of a book called *Jailbird* by the American author Kurt Vonnegut. It was, the review said, a novel about the forgotten man of the Watergate Affair writing his memoirs from prison. I'd never heard of Kurt Vonnegut before but the book sounded pretty interesting and so I headed off into town to buy it. I was living in Stafford at the time and it was not (and still isn't as far as I'm aware) the cultural capital of the world. Staffordshire County Council banned the showing of *Monty Python's Life of Brian* in all its cinemas in 1979, and in 1984 it advised its bookshops not to sell Raymond Briggs' brilliantly acerbic picture book *The Tin Pot Foreign General and The Old Iron Woman*.

Needless to say I couldn't find a copy of *Jailbird* anywhere. What I did find in a second-hand bookshop, though, was Kurt Vonnegut's 1969 novel *Slaughterhouse-Five*.

It changed my life. It changed the way I thought. It made me look at life in a completely different way.

But what's it about?

The best way I can think of to describe what it's about is to recall a memory I have of a book group I joined in the South of England back in the 1990s. When I say book group what I really mean is a gathering of literary snobs. There were about ten people in the group and they met each week and discussed the book they had been reading. The rules were that each person in the group got a turn in choosing a book. The members of the group were open to any kind of genre—or so they said. Their choice of reading ranged from pretentious unreadable prize winning books to ancient unreadable classics to *Anna Karenina*. When it came to my turn I chose *Slaughterhouse-Five* because I thought the group would benefit from reading something a little bit different.

They sounded very interested when I told them that the book was based on Vonnegut's own experiences as an American prisoner-of-war in Dresden. When the allies bombed it back to the stone-age Vonnegut and his fellow POWs were held in an underground slaughterhouse and the experience understandably deeply affected him. The novel's central character is Billy Pilgrim and Vonnegut writes himself in as a minor character. As I was explaining how, during the bombing of Dresden, Billy Pilgrim is unexpectedly kidnapped by aliens from the planet Tralfamadore, I noticed that everyone had stopped listening to me. All through the bit about Dresden they'd *oohed* and *aahed* and had been taking notes but as soon as I mentioned aliens they all put their pens down and closed their note books.

"I'm sorry Steve," the group leader said, "but we don't read science fiction in this group."

"That's right," said her husband, "we consider it childish and immature."

"But the rules of your group say that we are committed to reading all types of book," I reasoned, "and that all our choices should be read no matter what the genre."

"Not if it's science-fiction."

"But they burned this book in American universities because of the things he alluded to. It's one of the most influential books of all time. It ranks alongside books like *Catcher in the Rye*, *Catch-22* and *The Dice Man*."

"But it is still science-fiction," snapped the group leader, "and we *don't* read science-fiction"

"It's not really science-fiction. The sci-fi element is a metaphor for what was happening in America at the time. It's a humanist book."

I knew I shouldn't have said *sci-fi*. No matter how much I implored them to read the book, after I'd mention the term *sci-fi* they were just not prepared to listen to me anymore.

Science-fiction was bad enough—but *sci-fi*!

It was a shame because they might have picked up on some of the book's wisdom and maybe it might have changed their lives too. They were all getting on in years and Vonnegut's philosophy of life and death might have cheered them up a bit.

During his captivity Billy Pilgrim is taught that it would be silly to cry at someone's funeral because that person hasn't really died—he just *appeared* to die and each moment of his life—past, present and future—is still alive because those moments are all permanently fixed in time. The Tralfamadorians believed that it would be illusory to think that one moment followed another and that when that moment was gone it would be gone forever.

I think Kurt Vonnegut also believed that.

I know I do.

But none of that mattered to the book group.

The group leader turned to her devoted followers and asked, "Does anyone else have any *sensible* suggestions?"

"Why don't we read *Anna Karenina* again," someone said.

Regards
Stephen Mitchell

PS: The book you are about to read contains no elements of science-fiction.

to the memory of William Owen (1898-1973)

Above the fireplace in the front room of my grandparent's house, secured in a gilt-edged frame, a portrait of a young soldier held pride of place. He was dressed in a uniform bearing the insignia of the Royal Warwickshire Regiment. His square face was youthful and fresh and it framed an angular nose, beneath which a disarming smile beamed with optimism. He had thin eyebrows; they were barely visible, almost feminine and his eyes sparkled with mischief whenever you looked at them. The portrait was painted by some unknown artist using pastel colours on white silk. Concealed beneath the silk was the original photograph, taken in 1915, two days before the soldier's sixteenth birthday and three days before his departure to France.

THE TIN OF MEMORIES

I found the old *Quality Street* tin under my mother's bed when I was clearing out her flat and as I blew the dust of decades from its lid it immediately brought back a vivid memory of one Christmas from my childhood. The tin used to sit on top of a glass cabinet full of glass animals and only ever left its lofty perch once a day where its lid would be removed and the chocolates and toffees inside would be offered to family and friends (only one each, mind).

Aside from the paintings of Regency soldiers and their ladies that adorned the tin's curved edge, there was nothing else to indicate the treasures it contained and so when I removed the lid I was surprised to find a collection of eighteen photographs, all of which featured me in some form or other. I also found a photograph of my grandfather and a silk portrait that had been expertly copied from it, which was rolled into a narrow tube and fastened with a ribbon tied into a bow.

The first photograph that caught my eye was of a wedding party stood outside the doors of Blackpool Registry Office on a bitterly cold day in the February of 1965.

In the centre of the group is my grandfather. Although he's in his early sixties, he looks much younger; the black-and-white of the photograph can't disguise the mischievous sparkle in his eyes as he stands there in a double-breasted jacket with baggy high-waisted trousers. To the left of him is his wife, Edith. Much smaller than him, slightly built, but shapely, her hat casts a seductive shadow over her face and even in her advancing years she can still turn a few heads. The traces of beauty that attracted him to her in the first place are still visible on her high-cheekboned face. My mother is stood to the right of them clutching a bouquet of flowers. Blonde, although not natural, she's thirty years of age but looks much younger. Her right arm is outstretched, the fingers extended, left leg kicking in the air; she's pretending to be one of the showgirls she'd seen on the stage of the Winter Gardens the previous evening. She's hanging absently onto the arm of her new husband, whose grey suit looks second hand and a little shabby but his toupee is positioned so perfectly you wouldn't know it was there. Uncle Chas is stood next to him, his right hand closed into a fist; he scowls in the direction of the unseen cameraman. I'm knelt down in front of the group, eight years old and dressed in a horrible pageboy's outfit.

I took the box home with me and arranged the pictures into a rough chronological order and then stuck them down in a photograph album.

Each one was a permanent moment from my childhood, a short glimpse of the truth of my life that had been forever frozen in time.

It's the memories those moments triggered that were important because it was those distant events that made me who I am today.

I can remember a long way back, as far back as my father's last tender kiss on my cheek. When I was younger it was a hazy recollection, like the ghostly image on a blurred photograph, but as the years have rolled by that first memory of mine has become more focussed, more *real*.

Age has relentlessly crept up on me like moss on a dry-stone wall and over the years I've cherry-picked my moments of time. A moment here, a moment there—chosen at random from a memory rapidly losing its grip.

I know I can't change the *ending* of my life, but I can change the beginning and the middle; I've already done it several times. I do it by ruthlessly stealing other people's memories to selfishly improve my own.

Perhaps *my* first memory never happened the way I remember it and it's just a fiction that my mind has developed and embellished over the years.

A borrowed memory.

Everyone has them.

Someone will tell me tell me a story that will somehow fit neatly into my own life and as time moves on and I move away and I make new circles of friends and acquaintances, I steal that story and make it my own—my white lie becomes part of *me*, part of *my* life, and I tell my borrowed memory so many times that I end up believing it myself.

It has become *my* memory.

But that's just the way memories are—they are fickle; they change as often as the wind—they have their own life.

They are misleading.

Maybe my first memory is not my own.

Maybe it never happened at all.

But as I open the photograph album at its first page I can still remember the circular movement of my wooden livestock . . .

THE CIRCULAR MOVEMENT OF WOODEN LIVESTOCK

I remember the cows and sheep suspended from my ceiling, revolving slowly from light to shade; they danced, their shapes gliding across the wall, silhouetted by the street lamp outside my window, before their shadows retreated back to the safety of the dark corners of the room. I rocked my head from side to side and my gaze followed the gentle circular movement of my wooden livestock.

I looked around at the wooden bars that surrounded me. Everything was new even though I'd seen it all before.

My memory was not yet formed.

I had no notion of time.

I did what I always did when I required some attention. It was a primal function, an in-built survival mechanism, a latent memory thrust upon me from when I first gasped out of my mother's womb.

I started to cry.

After a short while I heard the sound of footsteps treading softly on the carpeted landing outside my door, and a few moments later a yellow ribbon of light crept slowly across the floor of the room. I pulled myself up on the bars of my cot and bounced up and down in gleeful anticipation.

As the man came closer I smiled and held out my arms, ready to be hoisted up in one fluid movement. But, instead he just laid me back down and covered me with my blanket.

"Back in your box, young man," he said softly. "It's way too early."

He leant over the side of the cot and planted a gentle kiss on my cheek. "I love you," he whispered.

Then he left the room, closing the door softly behind him, and was gone.

Forever.

The Law of Gravity

Each night when Granddad arrived home from work he would smile warmly at me and thrust his hand into his pocket and—like magic—would produce a dirty old sweet.

"What have we got here, then," he would say.

Gobstoppers, Black Jacks, Fruit Salads, Flying Saucers, Liquorice Sticks, Refreshers, Aniseed Balls, all found their way into the dark folds of his deep overcoat pockets.

"Anything broken?" he would ask Grandma.

"Not today," she would reply, casting a relieved glance at her treasured collection of glass animals.

They used the same words, the same rhythm of speech each night. It was something they did without even realising.

Mum and Granddad both worked for the Salwick Nuclear Energy Department, and while they were at work I was left under the watchful eye of my Grandma, who I wore to a frazzle with my boisterous behaviour.

We had moved there after my mother's marriage broke up and I only had a fleeting memory—a goodbye kiss on the cheek from an unknown father in that distant time.

By the time I was five my boisterousness had been replaced with extended bouts of nervous energy and so, in an attempt to calm me down, Grandma allowed me to hold one of her glass animals, but when she did she was always at my shoulder, hopping nervously from one foot to the other.

Her extensive collection of glass animals was kept in a tall, glass-fronted cabinet that stood on the back wall of the lounge. It was the focal point of the room, her pride and joy, and ordinarily I was not allowed within a mile of it.

As well as the manufactured animals encased in their glass shrine, my grandparents had three real ones—Shane, George and That Bloody Bird.

Shane, named after Grandma's favourite film, was an old dog, a cross (somehow) between a corgi and a German Shepherd. He had a problem with his bowels and seemed to spend most of the time releasing foul smelling odours into the room that he himself didn't seem able to smell.

Granddad often used Shane as an excuse for when he did the same.

"Has that dog farted again?" he would say, wafting his hand across his face.

Grandma, being uncannily sensitive in the olfactory department could easily distinguish between Shane's emissions and those of her husband. "Monkeys smell their own shit first," she would reply mysteriously.

Granddad always acted surprised when she displayed this amazing ability but he knew full well the reason why she was so perceptive—his farts didn't smell anywhere near as bad as Shane's.

George was named after Grandma's brother and was a huge white rabbit that spent most of his time sprawled out in front of the fire, nibbling at the corners of an old green rug. When he wasn't asleep he wandered about the house looking for anything green to eat. George only had one rule—green was edible—and he'd nibbled the bottom of the green curtains in the lounge; he'd eaten whole chunks out of

Mum's green dress when she was foolish enough to leave it lying on the floor, and when one of Granddad's workmate's came home with him for tea he left the house later that evening completely unaware that one of the legs of his green trousers was marginally shorter than the other.

At night George slept outside in a hutch next to a wire pen where That Bloody Bird lived. That Bloody Bird wasn't given a name because Granddad had brought it home earlier in the year to fatten it up and eat it for Easter. But when Easter came around the thing had grown into a monster, so large and fierce that no one, least of all Granddad, had the courage to step into its pen, let alone kill it. As the months went by That Bloody Bird became more and more aggressive, strutting around its domain like a mad king and attacking anyone who went near it.

"When are you going to kill that bloody bird, Bill?" Grandma asked him.

"Christmas," was his nervous reply.

Grandma was not the kind of person who tolerated idle promises and she nagged and nagged at Granddad to kill That Bloody Bird in time for the Christmas celebrations. Amazingly, he kept his word, although he did get one of his less squeamish friends to do the dirty deed, and That Bloody Bird did indeed find its way onto the Christmas table.

In life, That Bloody Bird had been the toughest turkey on the block, the toughest turkey in the history of tough turkeys. In death, it was even tougher. It was the stringiest, grisliest, foulest tasting turkey that ever walked the face of the earth. Rather than standing resplendent on the Christmas table surrounded by roast potatoes and brussel sprouts, it ended up being cast into the dustbin, providing a veritable feast for all the cats in the neighbourhood who were far less choosy.

After we'd eaten we sat in the front room listening to a programme about Father Christmas and the North Pole on the radio.

"Is Father Christmas real?" I asked Granddad.

"What kind of question is that?" he replied. "Who have you been talking to?"

"Deborah Delany says there no such person."

"Well, she's an eejit," said Granddad, his Irish accent returning for a brief moment. "What the hell does she know anyway? Of course there's a Father Christmas. How did you think you got all the presents you got this morning. We certainly can't afford them. What matters is if *you* believe in him." He paused and looked me straight in the eye. "Well, do you?"

"Yes," I said.

"Then that's all that counts. The magic is in you. You hold the key to his existence and as long as you believe and hold that magic close to you then the possibilities are endless. Don't you see that?"

I didn't see it but I said yes anyway because Granddad was the wisest man I knew.

Each year at Christmas Mum bought two tins of *Quality Street*—one for the family and the other for herself. She placed the family tin on top of the glass-fronted cabinet in the lounge and I was allowed to have one sweet a night, just before I went to bed.

"Can I have another one?" I always asked, to which Mum always replied, "No."

"Why not?"

"Be reasonable, will you, they have to last us all Christmas."

I was five—being reasonable was not a phrase that featured in my limited vocabulary and on Christmas Night, after gorging myself on the sweets and chocolates I had found in my stocking that morning, I went to bed. But greed got the better of me, and I waited until everyone had gone to bed before executing a cunning plan I'd been pondering over since the beginning of the festive season. I crept downstairs under cover of darkness like a highly trained commando. I sneaked into the lounge, lighter on my feet than the world's greatest cat burglar and climbed to the top of the glass-fronted cabinet with more tenacity than Edmund Hilary.

At this point it would be safe to assume that Isaac Newton's law of universal gravitation was an unfamiliar and abstract concept to me. And, by understanding this inalienable truth, it would be quite correct to surmise that, as I reached that Holy Grail of tins, the top of the glass-fronted cabinet was now considerably heavier than the bottom.

My knuckles started to turn white as I watched the top of the cabinet start to move away from the wall. I didn't know what was happening at first, but, as I turned my head to look around, the full horror of my predicament (closely followed by the floor and then the cabinet) hit me.

The noise created by a glass-fronted cabinet containing several hundred tiny glass animals crashing on top of a five-year-old boy is ear shattering, but, once the cabinet and its dismembered contents had settled, the silence that followed was even more deafening.

The next sound I heard was the thundering of bare feet rushing down the stairs, followed by the metallic click of the light switch. As bright light filled the room my eyes began to flicker and, just before I passed out, I felt the weight of the cabinet being lifted from my body.

When I regained consciousness, Mum and my grandparents were crouched over me in the wreckage that was once Grandma's pride and joy.

"The little bugger was after the Quality Street," said Mum, her voice loaded with annoyance.

"Just be thankful he's alright," said Granddad softly. "It could have been a lot worse."

"How could it be worse?" sobbed Grandma. "Look at all my animals."

The floor looked like a glass abattoir. The dismembered bodies of Grandma's treasured collection were everywhere. At first it seemed nothing has escaped, but on closer inspection it appeared that one animal *had* survived. It stood fiercely defiant in the middle of its shattered, fallen comrades.

It was a turkey.

Grandma took one look at it and, with a face that could have stopped clocks, crushed it under the merciless heel of her slipper. "A fine Christmas this has turned out to be," she grumbled, before stomping off up the stairs.

Granddad carried me to bed and as he covered me with a blanket he winked at me and from out of his dressing gown pocket he produced a dirty old sweet.

"Don't tell your mum," he whispered.

"Is it a secret?" I asked him.

"Yes," he said. "Now go back to sleep, there's a good lad."

Then he kissed my forehead and left the room, closing the door softly behind him.

I closed my eyes and, in those precious moments before sleep, I felt the law of universal gravitation working its invisible magic on me.

Fun With Effervescent Powder

Mum dragged me along to Bingo at the Mecca Ballroom once to 'keep her company'. It was the first and only time she ever did; I never really understood why I had to accompany her that night because she never spoke to me or allowed me to speak whilst a game was in play. I couldn't talk even when a game was over because the din was so all-encompassing I could barely hear myself think.

A deathly hush suddenly descended on the hall when the caller started each new game. Once he uttered the dreaded words, "Eyes down—look in!" I wasn't allowed to even breathe—if I coughed or whispered I got a dirty look from everyone in the hall, especially from the old woman sat opposite, who would screw her face up, making herself look like an old Kleenex tissue that had been found up someone's sleeve after a week of heavy use and I suspect that if she ever heard a pin drop she would demand that the pin and the person who dropped it be immediately removed from the premises and publicly flogged.

At the end of what seemed like an endless night everyone made their miserable way homeward, bemoaning the fact that they had less money in their purses than when they started and I got the impression that none of them had actually enjoyed themselves. My mother groaned and complained all the way home, mainly about the jackpot winner, calling her a "fat cow" and a "jammy bitch". "I'll bet she shits bloody diamonds when she goes t' toilet," was one of her more colourful descriptions. The fat cow or jammy bitch who had just won the jackpot, however, behaved like she had just won a million pounds and was about to be flown to a villa in Spain with her equally fat husband where they would spend the rest of their lives eating fish and chips and drinking *Watney's Red Barrel*.

The only other person who seemed to have any fun was the caller, who was allowed to shout, "Two fat ladies—Eighty-Eight!" Bingo callers today are not allowed to say that any more in case it upsets any ladies in the hall who happen to be overweight.

Generally my mother went to Bingo with my Grandma and Aunty Sylvia, who had a beehive hair-do and wore clothes that were ten years too young for her. I'd always assumed Sylvia was a member of the family but she was just my mother's best friend from her school days.

I remember one night when the three of them were out at Bingo and I was left at home with Granddad and we spent the night listening to the radio, drinking fizzy pop and scoffing liquorice allsorts.

Actually we didn't have any fizzy pop—we just had orange squash but after searching through the kitchen cupboards Granddad found a tin of *Andrews Liver Salts Effervescent Powder.*

"This'll do lad," he said, "a couple of teaspoons of this mixed with some orange squash will do the trick."

"Are you sure, granddad? It looks like medicine to me."

"No, it'll be grand; you'll see."

For those unaware of the Pharmaceutical Form and Clinical Particulars of *Andrews Liver Salts Effervescent Powder*, let me explain: it is a white free-flowing powder which effervesces on addition to water. It is recommended as a laxative and for adults the recommended dose is two level 10ml spoonfuls in one glass of water per day. For children the recommended dose is half that amount.

Therefore, after we'd shared a box of *Basset's* liquorice allsorts between us, which was then washed down with five or six glasses of Granddad's home-made fizzy pop, my stomach understandably began to gurgle and rumble. This gurgling and rumbling was quickly followed by the first of several hundred bowel-trembling farts that exploded out through the seat of my grey polyester trousers.

Granddad burst out laughing and then let out the longest, loudest fart I had ever heard in my life. At the time it was the funniest thing we had ever heard and we spent the rest of the evening farting and laughing until we lost all feeling in our cheeks and our sides ached. We had competitions to see who could fart the longest and who could fart the loudest. I discovered that if I lay on my back on the sofa and held my legs up in the air I could fart at will, and I used this newly-found skill to challenge Granddad to a game of *Name That Tune*, using farts instead of musical notes.

When Mum and Grandma returned home after their disappointing night at the Bingo they ran into a wall so thick with foul smelling odours they almost had to hack their way into the lounge with machetes.

"You dirty buggers!" Grandma screamed. "Get outside and shake yourselves."

We waited in the hallway, giggling and farting while Grandma fumigated the living room with air freshener and my mother complained about the fat cow who had won the jackpot again that night.

Millwater Germs

Maureen Millwater wore a pink plastic patch over her right eye that concealed an empty socket which, when the days were warm enough, would exude a pale green pus that seeped out from behind the patch and ran down her cheek like a tiny river of toxic waste. Covering her face was a mass of swollen spots that seemed to shift around like an army of red ants. Extreme myopia forced her to wear spectacles so thick her right eye looked like it belonged to a bush baby. Her teeth appeared to belong to someone four times her size, sprouting from her gums like the rocks of Stonehenge and setting her mouth into a permanent grimace. Her hair hung limply and greasily from her head, making it resemble a rugby ball adorned with a thousand strands of thin oily string.

Not to put too fine a point on it, Maureen Millwater was *hideous*.

Even her name, when spoken slowly enough (*Mmmiiiilllwwwaterrr*), sounded ugly.

I was eleven-years old at the time and a few months away from taking the Eleven-Plus exam. This exam was designed to separate the wheat from the chaff and, depending on your results, it determined if you were grammar school material or one of the thickies who were to be consigned to a secondary modern education.

Underachievement came naturally to me, and I fell easily into the second category. As far back as I can remember school and myself had very little in common—in fact, after completing my first day at *Rosehaven Primary School*, I was met at the gates by my grandma, who gave me a beaming smile and a hug and then asked if I had enjoyed myself. "Yes," I replied, smiling back at her, "but I don't think I'll go again."

During school hours Maureen was avoided like the plague but if, by chance, she happened to touch you, you were deemed to have Millwater Germs and the only way of getting rid of them was to pass them quickly onto someone else.

Two rules had to be observed when passing on Millwater Germs.

Rule 1: Millwater Germs cannot be passed back to the person passing them on by the person they'd been passed on to.

Rule 2: Millwater Germs cannot be passed on just by touch alone. A certain ritual should be followed. The infected person must rub his selected victim with back of his hand, then the flat of his hand, before saying with a grimace, "Yeeeerrrrch, you've got Mmmiiiilllwwwaterrr Germs!"

Only by strictly adhering to these two tried-and-tested rules could Millwater Germs be successfully passed on from one person to another.

By far the most terrible thing about Maureen was that her hideousness was absolutely impossible not to look at. She was so ugly eyes would be instinctively drawn to her, and new boys would stare at her, transfixed by her unbelievable ugliness.

One morning, when Maureen's good eye caught me staring at her in class, she gave me a little smile and waved her fingers coyly at me. I immediately looked away but found it extremely difficult not to look back. I could see that she was still looking at me with a doe-eyed (in the singular sense) expression. My classmates were sniggering behind their hands and I knew I was in trouble.

During morning playtime Maureen followed me around like a love sick puppy. Everywhere I went she seemed to be two steps behind. I couldn't get rid of her. I even ducked into the toilets and hung around in there for a few minutes hoping she'd get bored and wander off, but when I came out I found her outside waiting patiently for me.

I became so desperate to escape her that I joined in with one of the moronic games the other kids indulged in over playtime.

They played running games like 'Tig' and 'British Bulldog'.

Tig required one kid to play *It* and he had to run after the other kids until he caught one, at which point that kid would become *It*. In British Bulldog *It* stood in the middle and the rest of the players lined up at one end of the playground until a signal was given for them to charge to the other end. Whoever gets caught by *It* also becomes an *It* and this would go on until everyone was an *It*.

The hardier kids played the contact games like *Conkers*—a violent an aggressive game that required the conkers to be soaked in vinegar and then baked in the oven until they were as hard as rock. A hole was then drilled through the centre and the conker was attached to the end of a piece of knotted string. The object of the game was to smash your opponent's conker to pieces by swinging your conker at it with as much forward momentum as possible, an action which resulted in many bruised knuckles and black eyes.

Another contact game was *Ball Tag*—a particularly unpleasant and sadistic ball game that involved *It* throwing a tennis ball at you with such velocity that you'd be left with an ugly red mark wherever it struck you. If *It* had a particularly good aim *and* didn't like you then there was every possibility that you would spend the rest of the day in agony with shooting pains emanating from your testicles.

Then there was *Kiss Chase*—a running and contact hybrid that I was worryingly asked to play once in Senior School; my cause for concern was that boys and girls inhabited separate playgrounds.

Maureen Millwater asked me if I wanted to play Kiss Chase at lunch break. I gave her an emphatic no, but I still had to endure a whole hour of her following me around and grinning at me with her hideously toothy smile. She sat opposite me at the lunch table and grinned at me throughout the meal and, when my appetite had completely deserted me, she moved right up to me, smiled and said in her deep, gruff, almost manly voice, "I fancy you, Steve."

Oh God, I thought, she's got a deeper voice than my Uncle John!

The word *uncle* became a regular part of my vocabulary after my mother was divorced. As far as I was aware I only had one uncle, my mother's brother Charles, who everyone called Chas, but after she moved back in with her parents the number of uncles I was introduced to increased exponentially. Some I only met once, others two or three times. Uncle John was the latest and had been around for about six months. He wasn't as good-looking as the other uncles I'd met—he was bald and his nose had been broken at some point in his life, but what separated him from the rest of the pack was simple—he had a car. Mum didn't drive and had never expressed any interest in learning how to, but she was quite content to be chauffeured around by Uncle John.

I liked him when he was mum's boyfriend and, although my opinion of him changed after they were married, when Maureen Millwater was making advances towards me he listened intently, before roaring with laughter at my predicament.

I didn't say anything to Maureen after she told me that she liked me. I was terrified and all I could do was grunt at her and move away, hoping this rebuke might have the desired effect and put her off, but it only served to make her more determined. My lack of any kind of response (grunting excepted) had appeared to convince her that I was playing hard to get. They say that beauty is only skin deep and, underneath the veil of unbearable ugliness, Maureen was probably a really nice girl with a fascinating and pleasant personality. That, however, didn't alter the fact that I wouldn't have been seen dead with her under any circumstances.

I wasn't playing hard to get. I was playing *impossible* to get.

Whatever designs Maureen had on me needed to be quickly crushed and so, during afternoon playtime, I focused my mind on the difficult task of breaking the bad news to her in a subtle but firm way.

After summoning up the courage, I strode purposefully across the playground to confront her and tell her, in no uncertain terms, that any relationship she had in mind that involved me was completely out of the question and, as I advanced towards her, I saw her eye light up in dreamy anticipation.

"Hello," she said when I reached her, "I've been waiting for you.

"*Fuck off, you ugly cow!*" I screamed in a subtle, but firm voice, "*Stop following me around! I don't fancy you, and I never bloody will!*"

Maureen looked at me in horror and her lip started to quiver. "B . . . but you sent me a note," she sobbed.

"What? . . . *what?*"

She reached under her v-neck sweater and pulled out a folded piece of lined paper from the pocket of her school blouse. "Here," she said, unfolding it and handing it over to me, "I found it on my desk this morning."

I read through the declaration of love written on the note and immediately recognised the handwriting.

Apparently, Pete Webster, my *best friend*, thought that it would be extremely funny to fool Maureen into thinking that I fancied her. He also thought, judging from the smirk that had been plastered across his face all day, it would be rather amusing to watch her following me around like a love-sick puppy.

I smiled at Maureen and placed my hand on her shoulder. "This note's not from me, Maureen," I said. "It's from Pete Webster. He's the one that fancies you. He's always talking to me about you."

Her manner changed suddenly.

"Really?" she asked.

"Honestly—he'd never admit it to you—it's probably the reason why he sent you this note and signed it with my name. He just wants to worship you from afar. Haven't you noticed him looking at you in class? He's always doing it."

Maureen glanced over at Pete. "Mmmmm, he's quite nice isn't he." she said.

"Yeah. See you later Maureen."

I strolled over to the other side of the playground to where Pete was smoking a cigarette behind the bike sheds. The smile dropped from his face and he gave me a look of panic as I rubbed him once with the back of my hand and once with the flat of my hand before saying with a grimace, "Yeeerrrch, you've got *Mmmiiiilllwwwaterrr Gerrrmmmms!*"

On the Click of the Box-Brownie's Shutter

It had been raining all week; needle sharp, icy rain that speared its way into the bones. Stiff limbs ached and tempers frayed. Misery was absolute.

The wedding was a simple ceremony carried out with maximum efficiency and minimum fuss in a dismal and depressing Registry Office that boasted dirty yellow walls that complemented the Registrar's nicotine-stained fingers. After the hurried ceremony the hired photographer, a small, effeminate, fat man with piggy glasses herded everyone out onto the wet pavement and took pictures of us freezing to death.

"No! No! Over here! Over here! The light's no good over there," he ranted in a high-pitched voice as he minced up and down the pavement, directing us here and there in order to get a good picture. "How am I supposed to get a good composition when you're all over the place? I'm an artist, for God's sake!"

"Bloody arse bandit, more like," Uncle Chas growled. "I'd like to give him a bloody good kicking!"

With his fist clenched he went to move forward but Grandma slapped him across the top of his head with the flat of her hand and grabbed him by the scruff of the neck.

"Now, listen here, you little bugger," she hissed. "We'll have no trouble from you. Just because it's your sister's wedding day doesn't mean you can do what you bloody well like. So you'll bloody well behave yourself and you'll stay *sober*. And don't think that because you're bigger than me that I still won't give you a bloody good hiding. Now, have you got all that into your thick head?"

"Yes mum," said Chas meekly, and he begrudgingly did what the photographer asked.

The reception was held in the Halfway House, a large rambling pub at the top of St Anne's Road, and a less than appetising array of curled up sandwiches, pork pies, wrinkled sausages on sticks and soggy trifles were laid on for when we arrived. The buffet was tucked away in a dark corner of the pub, as if hidden there by the landlord to prevent it from being eaten (or, more likely, discovered). This culinary disaster was arranged on a large table covered in a white sheet that featured all manner of unusual stains.

"God, would you look at this," said Granddad, gingerly lifting a corner of the sheet. "It looks like King Kong's handkerchief. I'm not eating anything that's been on this bloody thing."

"Never mind the food," said Chas. "Where's Uncle George?"

George Pickup was Grandma's wayward brother and he had stood in the same corner of the Halfway House for the past forty years. It was his local and had been for as long as anyone could remember. George had served in the Royal Warwickshire's with Granddad during the Great War and afterwards, rather than return to his native Dublin, Granddad had stayed in Blackpool and married Edith, George's sister—my Grandma. During the Second World War George had remained in Blackpool for "essential services". Quite what those essential services were no one ever knew, but according to his sister all he ever seemed to do throughout the war was drink at the Halfway House. Maybe, she suggested in a letter to her husband who was somewhere in Italy, that he was essential in keeping the brewery business afloat while all the other men were away serving their King and country.

George was something of a legend in the drinking circles of Blackpool and from time to time a young pretender who thought he had the mettle would challenge him to a drinking contest. Like his father before him, George had a vast capacity for alcohol and these hopefuls came from as far away as Bolton to attempt to steal his crown. He saw himself like a gunslinger from the Wild West and all his contenders were left defeated, disappointed and usually in a comatose state.

He'd been stood at his usual place at the bar of the Halfway House when his niece had been getting married. He wasn't one for ceremony and he felt that he would have been wasting valuable drinking time hanging around the Registry Office looking bored. Besides, he was opposed to marriage and didn't want to be responsible for anyone but himself.

Over the years he'd grown to like, even depend, on that lifestyle. Bringing someone into his life would have been disastrous and would have upset the delicate equilibrium of his perfectly structured world. People could come in and out of his life, but they couldn't stay. He preferred visitors to permanent residents. He was the master of his own destiny and it would stay that way until he was found dead in his chair at home ten years later.

When he saw Chas heading towards him he knew exactly what was coming.

"Right then, George," said Chas. "Get the beers in. I'm going to drink you under the bloody table."

George rolled his eyes. "It's *Uncle* bloody George to you, lad," he said.

"Aye, alright then, if you say so."

"Pint for pint, it'll be," said George, calling the barmaid over.

"Just keep 'em coming."

George leaned over and whispered in the barmaid's ear. "This is my sister's daft son, Chas. Clear a space somewhere for him, will you, luv— he'll be unconscious in about an hour."

As she turned to go he added, "Oh, and you'd better fetch a bucket."

Aunty Sylvia was, as usual, tarted up to the eyeballs, her hair rigidly beehived, her eyelashes thick with mascara. She was sat at the bar sipping at a *Babycham*, crossing and uncrossing her legs provocatively as she watched Uncle Chas slip into drunken oblivion. She was smoking Menthol cigarettes because she thought they were good for her and made her look more sophisticated and attractive to men.

Two hours later Chas was reeling around the pub on unsteady feet leering at everyone through hooded stupefied eyes until he fell over and slipped into a dribbling unconsciousness.

Grandma tutted and tucked her arms under her breasts. "Look what my bloody brother's done to that daft apeth," she said to Granddad. "Go and sort him out will you, love."

"What do you want me to do about it?" whined Granddad, who was also feeling the worse for wear.

"I don't know. Sit him up in a chair or something. Anything. Just make him look respectable."

Granddad sighed and strode over to where Chas was slumped like a pile of old clothes ready for the Rag and Bone man. He began lifting him up on his own until Grandma shouted across the pub to him. "For God's sake, Bill, get someone to help you. You'll have a bloody heart attack doing that on your own, you daft bugger."

Granddad rolled his eyes and called me over.

We both picked Chas up who was amazingly still conscious but delirious, and carried him over to a chair where we dumped him down like a sack of potatoes. His head fell into the overflowing ashtray and clouds of fag ash flew up into the air. When we looked back we saw that he had an old dog end sticking out of his mouth.

"At least we know he's breathing," said Granddad. "Keep your eye on him, will you, lad."

I gave him a confused look.

"Just make sure he doesn't get into any more trouble."

Chas started to snort ash from the overflowing ashtray and after a short time he opened one eye.

"Alrigh' la'," he slurred.

"Granddad says I've got to keep an eye on you and stop you getting into trouble," I told him.

"Did 'e now?"

He looked around furtively and motioned for me to move closer to him. His face was now a deep grey colour from all the ash he'd been sleeping in and his breath smelled of stale tobacco and alcohol. He fished a damp dog end from the corner of his mouth.

"She's mad, you know," he whispered.

"Who?"

"Your mum. My bloody shister."

I shrugged my shoulders, unsure of what to say.

"Why?" I asked.

"Wrong'n," was his reply. He rolled his eyes. "Now, Ge' me a drin' then, there's a goo' lad; I can't seem to get up."

"Why don't you go home, Uncle Chas?"

"Go home?" Chas said. "I can' go home. I'm s'bess man. I'm shupposed to ge' a shag tonight."

He looked over at Aunty Sylvia and winked. "She'll do," he said.

Aunty Sylvia waved her fingers at him and smiled.

As I walked to the bar to get a glass of lemonade I saw the expression on Aunty Sylvia's face change from flirtatiousness to disappointment. She took a sip from her Babycham and lit up another Menthol cigarette.

When I looked back at Uncle Chas he was asleep and dribbling into the ashtray.

I wasn't sure what Uncle Chas had been talking about when he said "wrong-un" to me on that day but even as early as my mother and I moved out of my grandparent's house and into my stepfather's I knew instinctively that I would no longer be the centre of attention.

During the first few weeks of their marriage I could feel the family dynamic shifting in favour of nice Uncle John; only . . . he was no longer nice Uncle John. Like the parents in the film *Invaders From Mars* nice Uncle John seemed to have been replaced by something different and from that moment on nothing in my world would be the same again.

Chas had seen the warning signs long before the metallic click of the Box-Brownie's shutter captured forever that moment in 1965.

THE DEAD FOX
BY THE FIREPLACE

When John Watson became my stepfather my mother discovered that for years he had had an unhealthy interest in amateur boxing, which, by the time they married, resulted in the development of a rare skin condition that caused him to sweat all the time. Like a dog marking its territory, he left his smell wherever he went in the house. It was the kind of obnoxious stench that nineteenth century miners might have experienced a few moments after their canaries had fallen lifeless from their perches, an overpowering odour of salt-encrusted armpits, damp genitals and stale farts that lingered malignantly in the air long after he'd left the room.

His mother was a large, imposing woman who seemed to have a permanent scowl on her face and no sense of smell. Dressed entirely in black, her presence brought a feeling of gloom wherever she sat.

I thought she was mad. She seemed to have no concept of time, age, or anything for that matter and she disliked everyone except her son. She irritated me beyond measure.

The lounge, where she spent most of her days, was poorly lit and dingy. Everything in it looked old and worn. The wallpaper was of a curious design and when I looked at it for any length of time I could see faces in it, faces screwed up in painful torture, their eyes burning red in sunken sockets, their mouths open in silent screams. It was like stepping into a second-hand junk shop from some Dickensian nightmare, with John Watson's mother as its malevolent proprietor. And all the time, in the background, the dead fox by the fireplace kept a watchful, silent gaze over everything and everyone in the room.

"So how old are you?" Mrs Watson demanded of me.

"Eleven."

"Eleven what?"

"What? I don't know what you mean?"

"You should call me by my title. Eleven, Mrs Watson, that's what you should say."

"Why?"

"Because that's what people do in polite society."

She shifted her huge bulk around in her chair, "So, young man. Do you go to school?"

"Of course I do."

"Don't be snappy with me, young man or I'll show you the back of my hand."

"No you won't."

"You cheeky little bugger; I've a good mind to put you over my knee and give you a bloody good spanking."

"If you do that I'll tell the police and have you arrested."

She made a grunting sound and turned to her son. "Take this boy and sit him in a corner and don't let him speak to me again until you take him home," she said.

John Watson took hold of my hair and dragged me across the room. He threw me down onto a chair beside the fireplace. "Don't move," he said, pointing at me. "Don't speak. I'll deal with you later."

In Mrs Watson's dark and depressing house of loudly ticking clocks children were to be seen and not heard, only to speak when spoken to.

Everything in that room filled me with a sense of unease, the dead fox above all else. It held me in such a grip of fear that when I caught sight of it my buttocks clenched tight, my eyes bulged from their sockets and I broke out into a cold sweat.

The dead fox didn't just frighten me—it terrified me. It stood, encased in glass, to the left of the red brick fireplace. The years had not been kind to it. Its long snout was drawn back in a vicious snarl and sharp, white teeth showed clearly over the mottled, moth-eaten, faded red fur. But it was the eyes that terrified me the most. They looked real—alive—and no matter where I sat in that room the dead fox looked at me, its frozen snarl saying, *you're next, boy! You're next—just you wait and see!*

The more I tried to avert my eyes the more they were drawn back. It was as if some terrible, evil, restless spirit was trapped in its lifeless body, sealed forever by the taxidermist's needle and thread.

When the time came to go John Watson just pointed at me and said, "Out. In the car. Now."

He was silent in the car as we drove home but I could tell by looking at the back of his neck that things were not going to go well for me when we got there.

He was the first to reach the front door of the house and as he pushed it open he turned around and grabbed me by the collar and dragged me inside.

"You little fucker," he snarled at me. "Just who the fuck do you think you are?"

He picked me up off the ground, his hands closed tight around my collar and I could feel myself choking as the collar tightened around my neck. He held me in front of him and ran at the wall at the end of the hallway. Where was mum? I was thinking. Where was she? Why wasn't she doing anything about this?

The next thing I felt was my shoulders crashing into the wall. Fortunately it was made from two sheets of plasterboard and as my shoulders connected with the outer layer they smashed a jagged hole right through the wall. In a daze I could see the strip light on the ceiling and I realised that my head and shoulders were now in the kitchen.

"Oh my God," I heard my mother scream, "look what you've done to the wall!"

I waited for the inevitable beating that would follow but it never came. Maybe John Watson saw what he'd done and realised that it was wrong. Or maybe he just couldn't be bothered to follow it through. Either way I heard him tramp his sweaty way up stairs whilst my mother attempted to extricate me from the hole in the wall.

Later that evening she came into my room to see how I was.

"How do you think I am, mum?" I said. "He threw me through a wall."

"He's really all right, you know. I wouldn't have married him if he wasn't."

"Mum, he threw me through a wall."

"It were only plasterboard."

"It was still a wall, mum."

"I've had a word with him and he says it'll never happen again. He says that he's really sorry."

"If he's so sorry then why isn't he in here? Why is it you that's apologising for him?"

"Well, you know, it's a bit uncomfortable for him, after what he did, an' all."

"Be careful, mum. If he can do what he did to me . . ."

"Everything'll be all right. You'll see."

But I knew from that moment that everything would never be all right again.

My mother gave me a kiss on the cheek and quietly left the room, closing the door softly behind her.

BATMAN'S AUTOGRAPH

The *Tivoli* cinema stood in the centre of town, tucked away in a v-shaped block that also played host to *Yates's Wine Lodge*. Mum had taken me to see *Summer Holiday* there a couple of years earlier. She was a big fan of Cliff Richard, much preferring his bland wholesome style of rock'n'roll to the hip-swinging pelvic gyrations of a certain Mr Presley and therefore she was, despite her protests to the contrary, a bit of a square on the quiet.

The entrance to the cinema was hidden inside a covered shopping precinct within the block. Dimly lit and stinking of piss, it was the first stop for all the drunks that spewed out of the Wine Lodge in the early hours of the morning.

I was twelve when I saw *Batman—The Movie* at the Tivoli on a cold Saturday afternoon in the January of 1967. The seats were uncomfortable, the heating was non-existent and the place was a dump, but it was closer to where I lived and cheaper than the Odeon.

When I was seven, Granddad gave me a small collection of *Detective Comics* that he'd been given by a friend of his from work. His friend had told him that his own son had left home and had grown out of them. And so that evening instead of the usual dirty old sweet, granddad gave me something altogether more exciting; he introduced me to *Batman*.

I can still remember the first time I handled those comics—the feel and smell of the pulp paper on which they were produced, the brightly coloured artwork within their shiny covers, the brilliantly drawn panels of fast-moving action and the excitingly dynamic storylines. It must have seemed such a small thing for to him to do at the time, handing over a few unwanted second-hand comics to his grandson, but that one tiny, unsentimental act would set me off on a path that would turn me into a life-long lover (and collector) of comics. Even now, I can't understand *anyone* growing out of something so *wonderful*.

In 1966 *Batman* arrived onto the TV screens of Britain, and every Saturday and Sunday evening the youth of the nation would be transfixed, watching Adam West and Burt Ward playing the Caped Crusader and his young sidekick Robin. Saturday night's episode would end on a cliffhanger, with our two heroes caught in some fiendishly devious deathtrap, while the villains would all inexplicably leave them to their respective fates, from which they would then perform an unbelievably amazing escape at the start of Sunday night's episode.

The movie was released on the 16th December 1966 and with a bigger budget, it was able to feature the Bat-Boat and Bat-Copter, both of which appeared in a memorably hilarious scene featuring the Bat-Ladder, a rubber shark and a spray can of Bat-Shark repellent that the Caped Crusader just happened to be carrying in his utility belt. Audiences knew instinctively that Batman was climbing down the Bat-Ladder and not just some run-of-the-mill, bog standard ordinary ladder because attached to the bottom rung was a printed sign that read *Bat-Ladder*. As if all that wasn't enough for Bat-fans around the world, the movie contained *all four* of the major villains from the series; Caesar Romero as *The Joker*, Burgess Meredith as *The Penguin*, Frank Gorshin as *The Riddler* and Lee Merriwether (replacing Julie Newmar) as *Catwoman*.

I was in Bat-Heaven!

In the June of 1967 an advertisement appeared in the *Fylde Gazette* announcing the arrival of Batman and Robin in Britain. Along with the Batmobile, Adam West and Burt Ward had arrived on our shores to promote the second series of *Batman*.

Granddad pointed out the advert and my pupils dilated rapidly when I read that they would be signing autographs in *Lewis' Department Store* in the town centre that very weekend. I immediately showed the advert to my mother, who told me that there was no way on earth she was going to traipse all the way into town when she didn't need to do any shopping. She could see the desperation on my face and still she refused to take me, even after I had repeatedly asked her.

Grandma and Granddad were both busy that weekend so there was no one who could take me. "I'll go on my own, then," I said defiantly.

"You will *not* go on your own, *Stephen!*"

That was her final word on the matter and I knew she was serious because she had called me Stephen—in *italics*.

Batman and Robin were there for just *one day* and during the days leading up to the event my selfish mother dug her heels in and flatly ignored my increasingly pathetic pleading.

There was no one to accompany me into town and so there was nothing else for it; I had to defy my mother and go on my own without telling anyone.

What could possibly go wrong?

Lewis's Department Store was hot and muggy and a crowd of people were clamouring and shoving their way forward, trying to get a glimpse of the Caped Crusader. I was rake thin, and so able to scramble between the legs of the awe inspired crowd and reach the front with no problem. I was dumbstruck when I reached my exalted position and when I held out my hand Adam West shook it and pressed a small scrap of paper into my sweaty palm. I carefully unfolded the white square and gazed in adoration at the autograph.

I thought, *Wow!*

Nothing else.

Just *Wow!*

Then I was pushed and jostled back by the enthusiastic crowd.

But the pushing and jostling didn't stop and an unexpected dig of someone's elbow in the small of my back sent me crashing to the floor.

I slid along its polished surface until my head hit the side of a wooden shop display and I felt a sharp stab of pain in my neck. At first I thought nothing of it, but then I heard a woman's voice screaming hysterically, *"Oh My God! He's bleeding!"*

I instinctively brought my hand up to where the pain was. As I did this I felt something warm running over my fingers and down into the sleeve of my shirt. When I pulled my hand away it was covered in blood. Now I'm not good with blood, especially my own, and I tend to go into shock until someone qualified reassures me that I'm going to be all right and so therefore my head started to swim, a sudden dizziness overcame me and then I passed out.

The next thing I knew I was on a stretcher being jogged up and down by a couple of blue-suited ambulance-men. We were in the basement car park of the store, heading for a waiting ambulance. Through watery vision I could see the *Batmobile* standing silently over on the far side of the dimly lit car park.

"What do you think of that, then, kid?" one of the ambulance-men asked. "How would you like to go to the hospital in that?"

Bugger the Batmobile, I thought, *what's mum going to do when she finds out about this?*

With the siren wailing, the ambulance sped through the busy streets until it reached the ugly sprawling mass of red bricks and concrete that was Victoria Hospital. The vehicle screeched to a halt and the doors flew open. Strapped to a stretcher trolley, I was hurtled down long corridors and round sharp, blind corners, faster than a speeding bullet.

In an examination room a white-coated, kindly-faced doctor poked, prodded and scrutinised me. I was surrounded by space age looking equipment that appeared to have been borrowed from the set of *Star Trek.*

"Stitches," I heard the doctor say, softly. "Have you informed the parents?"

"The mother's on her way."

"Now then, son," the doctor said, turning to me, "you're going to need a few stitches, and because you're twelve you're old enough to have them put in without a general anaesthetic."

All the moisture in my mouth suddenly evaporated and a wave of self-pity swept over me. I looked at the doctor with a mixture of terror and confusion in my eyes.

"Now, don't be alarmed. You're a big lad now. We're going to give you a local anaesthetic. That just deadens the area where you've been hurt. Trust me, you won't feel a thing. We can give you a general anaesthetic that will knock you out if you like, but it's not advisable. Anyway, only sissies and girls have general anaesthetic. You don't want all your friends at school thinking you're a sissy, do you?"

Yes! Yes! I thought. *I do! I do! I do want them to think I'm a sissy!*

"Honestly, the stitches won't hurt. You'll just feel a tingling sensation at first and after that you won't feel a thing."

He lied. There may not have been any *physical* pain—but psychologically it was agony. At that moment I didn't see the kindly-faced, soft spoken doctor. I saw a maniac and all I could think of as the needle wove its way in and out of my skin was: *You fucking liar. You fucking fucking liar!*

Mum arrived a few minutes after I'd been sewn up and found me looking sorry for myself in the recovery room. My obvious discomfort had no effect on her mood whatsoever because she had traipsed all the way into town without needing to go shopping—and she was *furious*.

"What did I say to you?" she thundered.

I had to think of something fast and it had to be plausible. "Err . . . I came into town with . . . err . . . Pete Webster and his mum and . . . err . . . we got separated . . . err . . . and err . . . I fell over and . . . err . . . cut my neck open."

The doctor gave me a scornful look, but he didn't say anything.

"Serves you bloody right, then," Mum said, as she grabbed hold of my ear and dragged me out of the recovery room.

When we got home we had jam sandwiches for tea and, as I stuffed one into my mouth, I reached forward and pressed the large bakelite button on the television and waited for the old black and white, tube driven monster to warm up.

I was just in time. It was a new adventure. A new story. A different villain, and I remember thinking, just before the doorbell rang, I hope The Joker's in it this week.

As the sound and picture merged and the fuzziness disappeared, and the familiar *Na-Na-Na-Na-Na-Na-Na-Na Na-Na-Na-Na-Na-Na-Na-Na* signature tune began to fill the room, I heard my mother call to me from the hallway. "*Stephen!*" she yelled. "Me and Mrs Webster would like a word with you about what happened this afternoon!"

I opened my mouth to say something but in the random access memory of my brain I could only find four words that seemed suitable.

"Don't tell John Watson," I whispered.

Growing Up
Behind The Toilets

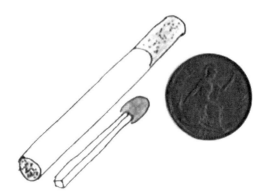

"I don't know, Pete," I said defensively.

"Aw, go on, they're dead good."

"Well . . ."

"It makes you bigger."

"Does it?"

"Yeah, and my sister likes boys who smoke."

I was offered my first cigarette behind the toilets in the playground of Highgrove Secondary Modern. It was an untipped *Players Weight* (cigarettes that now, sadly, no longer exist because of their extremely high tar content, each pack seemingly containing enough of the stuff to fix every pothole up and down the length of the Golden Mile).

All the flat-chested girls from Primary school began to grow up at Highgrove and by the time I was fourteen I would fix a fascinated stare at their developing breasts in the classroom or watch longingly as they jiggled around whenever the school bus went over a bump in the road. I'd had a secret crush on Pete's older sister for some time. She was sixteen, two years older than me, and I was barely aware of what was happening around me whenever she stood opposite me on the bus.

One day, on the way home from school, I was staring absently at her blouse, wishing that I'd sent away for the X-ray specs I'd seen in the *Superman* comic I'd bought the week before. I stared harder and harder, trying to create my own X-ray vision, to see through her white blouse and the white lacy bra underneath, to feast my eyes on those dark, organ stop sized nipples that Pete had told me about.

Then I heard her voice. "Steve," she said.

I looked up in wonder. She had spoken to me. I felt a surge of adrenaline rush through my body. It was the happiest moment of my life. She had spoken *to me*. I was in heaven. "Yes," I answered in dreamy anticipation.

"Fuck off and look somewhere else, will you!" she said.

I turned away quickly and looked out of the window in embarrassment.

That morning, behind the bike sheds at school, I snatched the cigarette from Pete and sucked on it, holding the smoke in my mouth for a few seconds before releasing it.

"No, not like that, *stupid*," said Pete. "You're supposed to inhale the smoke. It tastes better that way. Look . . . *like this*."

He snatched the cigarette from my fingers and took a long drag from it, inhaling the smoke into his lungs, before blowing it out through his mouth and nose. He handed the cigarette back to me and I took a drag, drawing the smoke deep into my lungs.

My eyes were the first to go—they started to water and I couldn't focus on anything. I felt light-headed and sick—everything around me was spinning. I was spinning. Spinning and sweating—it felt like sweat was dripping out of every pore of my body.

I felt like I was about to pass out.

It was horrible.

It was disgusting.

It was the single most repulsive thing I'd ever experienced in my entire life.

"Well?" asked Pete, impatiently, waiting for me to regain my composure.

"Fan-tas-tic!" I said.

There was a newsagent across the road from the school and I could buy a single *Park Drive* and a match for a penny. After I'd purchased my contraband I'd go around the corner to a side street and hope the wind didn't blow out my match as I was lighting up.

Mum thought cigarettes were disgusting and would quite possibly have murdered me if she'd caught me smoking one, and so I hid my contraband in a box under a shelf in the shed outside. She hated smoking because both her parents smoked, as did her younger brother Chas and in fact it was Chas and my grandparents who kept me supplied in cigarettes once I had become addicted to them. Therefore, I didn't think it was disgusting. It made me feel big.

And besides, girls liked boys who smoked.

Especially ones (I was unreliably informed) with big tits.

Maybe, I thought, I would appear more attractive to Miss McLellan, our sexy history teacher, if I smoked?

As I took another drag from that first cigarette and felt the powerful nicotine rush hit my brain I could hear, as I reeled with dizziness, the unmistakable *thrap-thrap-thapping* of Deborah Delaney wanking Edward Etherington off in the toilets behind me.

Edward Etherington, was the school bully.

William Beck, who was year below him had recently been elevated to the position of class bully and would therefore spend his lessons bullying whoever he decided to bully that week. He usually did it on a rotational basis, so that no-one in the class felt left out. However, once he was outside in the playground he immediately became one of Edward Etherington's toadies.

That week it happened to be my turn to be bullied by William Beck. He was bigger than me by about six inches—and he was broader. Unfortunately he was not a professional bully like Edward Etherington and his attempts at bullying in the classroom were at the very most annoying.

He *was* annoyingly annoying but no matter how annoyingly annoying he was, at the end of the day he was just simply annoying.

And so after three days of him flicking paper clips at me and whacking me on the back of the neck with a ruler I'd had enough.

"Right," I said, pointing a finger at him, "I'll fucking see you after school."

"Oh, yeah?" he said.

"Yeah," I replied.

"Oh, really?" he said.

"Really," I replied.

"Yeah?"

"Yeah."

"Yeah?"

"Yeah."

This exchange of "Yeahs?" and "Yeahs" went on for about four minutes until someone announced: "Three-thirty outside the back gate."

That sealed it. I didn't really want to have a fight and I suspect William Beck didn't either, but there was no backing out now.

At three-thirty outside the back gate of Highgrove Secondary Modern School I met with William Beck for what appeared to be the fight of the century. A huge crowd had gathered there shouting "Fight! Fight! Fight!" and as we approached each other they encircled us like Red Indians around a wagon train.

At first it was just posturing. "Come on, then!" he said.

"No, you come on!"

"I said it first."

"So what?"

Then we started lunging punches at each other and although I was fast on my feet his fist was the first to connect. He punched me squarely in the face and it was in that moment of agony that I knew I would never be able to beat him—not in a fair fight anyway.

With tears in my eyes I decided to change my tactics.

His next swing was wild and I was able to duck under his arm, reach up and grab hold of his head. As I pulled his head down I clamped my mouth onto his ear lobe and bit down as hard as I could. I heard him screaming as my top and bottom teeth were scraping against each other and I could taste blood in my mouth.

The adrenaline rush that followed made me increase the pressure until the pain in his ear got so bad that his knees buckled and he crumpled to the ground. Once he was there I used my feet to finish him off—I was in a frenzy and I would probably have kept on kicking him until I'd killed him if my friends had not dragged me away from him and calmed me down.

I slumped down on the pavement by the side of the road, my head between my legs, and I started to cry.

When mum and John Watson returned home from work that evening I explained to them what had happened and I was told not to worry. When the police arrived John Watson told them that he would deal with me later—but all he did was share a can of beer with me and congratulate me on my victory.

But if this was what victory felt like, then why did it feel so bad?

I was suspended from school for two weeks and I took that time to make amends. I went to see William Beck at his home. He answered the door and stood in front of me in silence with his bruised and scarred face.

"I've come to say sorry," I said, breaking the silence.

He thought about this for a moment until he eventually said, "I started it."

He invited me in. Like my mum and John Watson, his parents worked and left him at home to fend for himself. It was only then that I discovered that he had been suspended from school as well and so we talked and discovered we had a lot in common—comics, films, books, smoking, girls—and we became friends.

In the aftermath of our fight I came to realise that I had directed all my anger and rage at William Beck and he hadn't really deserved it. He was just another kid who was trying his best to survive each day in a big scary school.

And once we were both allowed back at Highgrove we would sneak off behind the toilets at break and, with Pete, we would smoke cigarettes and talk about girls with big tits.

MR TWATKINSON

No-one at Highgrove Secondary Modern School knew how Mr Edward Atkinson had gained employment as a geography teacher as he was wholly unsuitable for the task of educating teenage boys in any subject at all. One rumour suggested that the headmaster, Mr Bates, had been so impressed by Mr Atkinson when he turned up for interview dressed in the traditional uniform of a geography teacher— comfortable brown slip-on shoes, corduroy trousers, check shirt with plain tie and brown jacket complete with leather patched elbows—that he offered him the job without a moment's hesitation.

He began teaching in the autumn term of 1968 and right from the start, right from the very moment he introduced himself to his first class of teenage boys, his card was marked, he was doomed to failure and he would forever be referred to by the boys as Mr Twatkinson.

Mr Twatkinson spoke in a high-pitched nasal whine which, although initially amusing, soon became irritating and then eventually annoying. He was one of a new breed of teachers who abhorred corporal punishment but didn't carry the necessary authority to control a class full of teenage boys with raging hormones and bad attitudes.

He tried everything to befriend us. He told us jokes; he told us 'funny' stories about teacher training; he dropped the names of pop groups he thought we liked into his lessons. His jokes all fell flat; his stories were received with stony silence and his pop music references were revealed to be shallow, desperate attempts to connect with teenage boys who thought that anyone over twenty-five years old was ancient and knew nothing about anything.

After a few weeks we decided that he was just pathetic and therefore we unanimously voted to torture him mercilessly at every opportunity.

Here are five ways in which we tortured Mr Twatkinson:

1. We filled our pens with ink from the ink-wells on our desks and then splattered the ink all over his jacket when his back was turned.
2. One side of the class started to hum, a soft barely perceptible hum, but a hum nonetheless. This carried on until he moved over to that side of the class to attempt to discover where the strange irritating humming noise was coming from, at which point that side stopped humming and the other side started.
3. We chewed on pieces of paper until they were like *papier mâché* in our mouths. These would then be rolled into balls and then hurled at the blackboard when his back was turned.
4. We went into his classroom half an hour before the lesson started and hid all the geography text books and placed a drawing pin under the cushion of his seat.
5. Some of the class kept him talking at his desk at the end of the day by asking him pointless and inane questions whilst one member of the class lit a *Standard Fireworks Volcano* on one of the back desks, at which point everyone, with the exception of Mr Twatkinson, left the room.

During the winter term we noticed that on cold days he would walk around for about ten minutes before sitting on the hot radiator under the window. He would sit there for two or three minutes, warming himself up before he continued with the lesson.

Two of us sneaked into his classroom about twenty minutes before our Geography lesson was due to start and smeared the contents of a large tub of *Vaseline* over the radiator.

As the lesson started we couldn't concentrate on anything he said due to the anticipation of what we thought was going to follow.

When he eventually sat down on the radiator the *Vaseline* had reached a temperature that was not dissimilar to that of boiling oil. It only took a few seconds for it to seep through to his underpants, at which point he screamed and jumped so high into the air it exceeded all our expectations.

He never did suspect us, thinking instead that it was a fault with the radiator.

Our greatest triumph, however, came on the morning Graeme Webb turned up to school carrying a large canvas bag. Geography was first period after lunch, but Graeme would not reveal the mysterious contents of his bag until we arrived in Mr Twatkinson's empty classroom ten minutes before the lesson was due to start.

"Look what I borrowed from the garage," he whispered, lifting the black object out of the bag.

"What is it?" someone asked.

"It's a car battery, stupid" said Graeme.

"But what are you going to do with it?"

Graeme pulled out two thick electrical cables with clamps at each end.

"Watch this," he said. He attached one end of each cable to the terminals on the battery and then brushed the two other ends together. Everyone moved back a few inches when a crack of electricity split the air and sparks flew from the metal clamps.

"Ooooooooooooooooo," everyone said.

Graeme attached the two cables to the door handle of the classroom and moved back to his desk. We all followed suit and sat quietly waiting for Mr Twatkinson's approaching footsteps.

Mr Twatkinson was never late for his classes and this day was no exception. He arrived dead on time and through the windows of the classroom we could see that he was chatting to the headmaster, Mr Bates (who we all called Master Bates behind his back), as he gripped the handle on the other side of the door.

The electrical current that charged through the door handle sent him into, what I can only describe as, convulsions of an epileptic nature, and as his gripped tightened he started to scream.

Master Bates looked on in disbelief. "What's the matter, man," he said. "Pull yourself together, for God's sake."

Mr Twatkinson turned painfully to the headmaster and through clenched teeth, groaned, "Help me."

Master Bates took hold of Mr Twatkinson's arm and was immediately blown back by the force of the electrical charge and he collapsed onto the neatly mown grass of the quadrangle, his body twitching and his arms punching into the air.

It was only then that Graeme crawled to the door and unclipped the cable that was fastened to the door handle. As soon as the electricity was cut off Mr Twatkinson slumped to the ground, his whole body convulsing in front of us. Graeme returned the battery to its bag and hid it in the cupboard that contained all the items of contraband Mr Twatkinson had confiscated from us in previous Geography lessons.

By this time Master Bates was back on his feet. He looked confused until he saw us looking out of the window of the classroom. We were all trying to keep straight faces but it was difficult and some of us started to laugh. The expression on the headmaster's face turned from confusion to anger and he marched purposefully towards the door. He placed the flat of his hand against the door handle, before he grabbed hold of it and kicked the door open. He stepped over Mr Twatkinson's still twitching body, entered the classroom and bellowed, "*You lot have finally cooked your goose!*" He pointed his finger at us and swept his arm across the room. "*I know you lot had something to do with this,*" he continued to bellow, "*and I will bloody-well find out who is responsible! If the person who did this has not come forward and owned up by the end of the day I will cane the lot of you in front of the whole school in assembly tomorrow morning! You can trust me on that!*"

He never did find out who did it. Nobody came forward and admitted to it and nobody got caned in front of the whole school the next day. The problem with empty threats is that when their bluffs are called that's all they ever are or ever will be.

The odd thing about the whole thing is this—I *remember* Mr Twatkinson convulsing on the ground after receiving an electric shock. I *remember* Master Bates trying to help him and being electrocuted himself. I *remember* it all, even though I have been reliably informed on a number of occasions that a car battery attached to a metal door handle would never produce the effects I have just described. And if I *remember* this event so well, then why isn't it true? Is it a borrowed memory or have I just made it up somewhere along the line? I have no idea where it came from, but if it is a fiction created by my overactive imagination then it does make me feel less guilty about the torture we arbitrarily dished out to Mr Twatkinson on a daily basis.

Thank You, Sir

Discipline! Discipline! Discipline!

That was Mr Geoffrey Bates' motto. He was a former Guards officer and he ran Highgrove Secondary Modern School like an army training camp, barking orders at everyone who came within his radar. No walking on the grass! No hanging around the quadrangle! No running down the corridors! No standing around with hands in pockets! No electrocuting Geography teachers! No talking! No whispering! No breathing!

The British Army had been his life and he therefore actively encouraged all school leavers to make it theirs. "Think of it, son," he would tell them, "The travel, the adventure, the camaraderie . . . the *discipline*!"

The school covered an area of about a quarter of a mile and consisted of several older buildings connected to each other by a series of more modern glass and steel structures. If the whole complex were to be viewed from above it would probably have resembled a monstrous, badly constructed spider's web. At its centre was the assembly hall, where each morning Master Bates would conduct assembly in his usual brusque manner.

He was mid-way through his morning oration when he was interrupted by a shrill, moaning wail that emanated from the back of the assembly hall. This was closely followed by what sounded like a large sack of potatoes being dropped from a great height onto the highly polished parquet floor.

Master Bates ran his fingers down his regimental tie, straightened his jacket, placed his hands on his hips and said, in a slow and deliberate voice, "Will someone *please* pick Patterson up, take him outside and give him some air."

Then, as an afterthought, he added, "And bring a mop back with you"

Four of us picked Martin up by his arms and legs and carried him out of the assembly hall, where we dumped him unceremoniously by the double doors, like a victim of the bubonic plague.

"Bloody softy," moaned Edward Etherington.

Martin Patterson was the school fainter—he found it difficult to stand up for long periods at a time, at which point his mind would go blank, he'd fall asleep on his feet, have a nightmare and then faint.

Noisily.

There was always a fight to decide who would carry him outside as it meant missing the rest of assembly and the hymn that followed, which was invariably *Onward Christian Soldiers* or *Jerusalem*, two of Master Bates' favourites. The rest of the staff, seated behind Master Bates on the raised platform would only pretend to sing, mumbling their way through the words whilst attempting to keep time with the tinkling, out-of-tune piano. Master Bates, on the other hand, sang with gusto, his chest moving in and out like a huge set of bellows, his mouth opening and closing like a giant fish starved of oxygen. The assembled children in the large hall would stand and snigger at him, or sing the wrong words (usually rude), watching with embarrassment as he bellowed out the hymn like a demented opera singer.

With almost radar-like precision Master Bates always seemed able to pinpoint the boys who changed even one syllable of his beloved hymns, and the guilty parties would be instructed to wait outside his office after assembly. Once there they would be marched in one by one and given five strokes of the cane across their left palms (or right palms if they happened to be left handed).

"Say thank you, boy," Master Bates would say, after administering his punishment.

"Thank you," the boy would reply.

"Thank you what?"

"Thank you, sir."

Martin Patterson never got the cane on account of his delicate constitution (and the intervention of his mother) and so consequently he only ever got a tepid telling off if he ever stepped out of line.

Martin's father had left his wife before Martin was born on account of his wife's increasingly strange behaviour and he never returned home owing to the fact that he was killed soon afterwards in a freak motorway accident. Mrs Patterson had insisted that the child growing inside her was not Mr Patterson's but the product of an alien who had kidnapped and then impregnated her while he had been away on a business trip. After Martin was born things became more complicated when Mrs Patterson convinced herself that Martin was not her child at all and that a vengeful maternity nurse had switched him at birth with another similar (albeit not alien) baby. She believed that her alien child was being cared for by an unwitting surrogate mother and as a result her behaviour became more bizarre and obsessive.

Mrs Patterson always collected Martin from school in case his real parents turned up to claim him and when they arrived at home she would double lock all the doors and windows, hermetically sealing herself and her precious child in the house until the following morning when she would accompany him to school. She poured love on Martin all the time because she was convinced that each day might possibly be the last she would have with him. She also issued strict instructions to Master Bates and his staff that she would get the police involved if they ever so much as raised a finger to her boy and that they should never *ever* put him in a situation where he would feel in any way uncomfortable.

As a direct consequence of Mrs Patterson's request Master Bates strode into our classroom after assembly one morning, narrowed his eyes, placed his hands on the red leatherette of the desk and said, "I want one of you lot to look after Patterson while everyone else is in assembly."

"I'll look after him, sir!" I cried, thrusting my hand high up into the air. "I'm his best friend."

I was lying, of course. Martin Patterson wasn't my best friend at all. I didn't even like him and, as Master Bates graciously accepted my gallant and apparently unselfish offer, I could see Martin visibly shaking.

I could have handled the enormously responsible job of looking after Martin in two ways:

1. I could actively and diligently monitor him and make mental notes of anything unusual about his behaviour so that I could report it to Master Bates upon his return from the assembly hall.
2. I could utilise my position of power over Martin by spending my assembly-free time constructively and mercilessly mentally abusing him.

I unhesitatingly opted for the second of those two choices.

I called him names like *Mong* and *Spaz-brain* and did flamboyant impressions of his regular and embarrassing fainting fits. "Hey, Spaz-brain," I'd say, "who's this?" Then I would moan loudly and crash to the floor, and all Martin could do was sit at his desk in abject misery, trying unconvincingly to make it look like he was laughing along with me and my cruel antics.

All good things eventually come to an end, and my reign of mental torture ended abruptly one morning when I misjudged one of my falls and cracked my head open on the corner of a desk, knocking myself out into the bargain. Until this point Martin hadn't breathed a single word to any of the teachers about how I'd been treating him while they were mumbling to the words of *Onward Christian Soldiers*. But, as I was being rushed to Victoria hospital to have the back of my head shaved and stitched, Martin spilled the beans.

He told Master Bates *everything*.

I was kept in hospital overnight for observation and when I returned to school the following day I was expecting to receive a good deal of sympathy for my unfortunate accident.

But instead, I had to say, "Thank you, sir," to Master Bates.

CHRISTMAS WITH RODGERS & HAMMERSTEIN

The smell of fireworks was still hanging in the air when they started to arrive.

With faces shrouded in balaclavas, they lurked malevolently in the shadows waiting for the right moment to strike. Tightly knit and well disciplined they leaped over walls and hedges with military precision to bombard the neighbourhood with song.

When the carol singers descended on us their primary aim was not to spread Joy to the World or Peace on Earth or Goodwill to All Men.

Their primary aim was to make money.

They did, however, possess one serious, fundamental flaw in their nocturnal, mercenary activity.

They didn't know any carols.

Those that did only seemed to know one—*Silent Night*—and most of *them* only knew the first four lines of it. The less experienced groups simply repeated the first four lines of the carol over and over again until they got bored and wandered off into the night muttering obscenities to each other. The experienced ones were more determined and, upon reaching that unremembered fifth line, would move effortlessly into an excruciating medley of songs from the back catalogue of Richard Rodgers and Oscar Hammerstein III. The residents of the street cowered fearfully in the dark corners of their houses whenever they heard their doorbells ring but the carol singers just kept at it, night after night, endlessly singing until the owners of the besieged houses eventually cracked and coughed up some money.

They were ruthlessly efficient.

John Watson was dozing on the couch, half-watching the flickering images that danced out of the black-and-white tube driven monster in the corner of the room. The television was always turned down low at this time of the year so the approaching footsteps of marauding carol singers could be heard more clearly.

Mum was sat beside him reading the Christmas issue of *People's Friend* while she fed one chocolate after another into her mouth. She was eating chocolates because she wasn't knitting. When she wasn't eating chocolates she would knit clothes that always ended up being stuffed away in cupboards or at the bottom of wardrobes, out of sight and out of mind. Her ugly, misshapen jumpers were the talk of the street, always in hushed tones and never within her earshot.

Granddad was over in the corner leafing through *Selected Essays and Journalism* by George Orwell. He didn't share Orwell's belief in socialism and he wasn't really reading the book—he was just filling his head full of information before Sylvia arrived.

Grandma was sat next to the electric fire, smoking a *Player's No 10* cigarette, or *Coffin Nail* as Granddad called it. She had a glass of sherry in her free hand and her corned-beefed legs were swaying to the rhythmic sound of her mutterings as she stared blankly at the coloured lights attached to the sparse wire branches of the imitation Christmas tree.

"For God's sake, stop muttering, will you!" John Watson growled.

"I wasn't muttering," snapped Grandma.

She had secretly made it her vocation in life to be utterly unpleasant to him at every possible opportunity and whenever he asked her what she was muttering about she just shrugged her shoulders and treated him to one of her enigmatic smiles which *convinced* him that she *was* muttering things about him. When she saw that her muttering *was* irritating him she muttered all the more, only louder.

Once, he caught her muttering behind the daily newspaper, which she held fully open and upside down in front of her. When he commented on the fact that the paper was the wrong way up she just smiled sweetly and said, "I know, Captain Thin Lips, and you've just walked into my clever trap."

John Watson knew there was no point in pursuing the subject of whether Grandma was or wasn't muttering, so he left it there and went back to watching the television.

"And a Merry Christmas to you, you miserable bugger," said Grandma, raising her glass to her lips.

John Watson held a special place in his heart for Christmas because he hated every minute of it. He hated the expense and the false good cheer and the cold and especially the carol singers.

The sound of rapping knuckles on the front door broke the uncomfortable silence that followed Grandma's less than festive toast. There were two short raps followed by three longer ones. This was the secret code given only to family and friends so John Watson could distinguish them from the carol singers who he knew were preying on the street.

"Who's that?" Grandma asked.

"How the bloody hell should I know," said John Watson. "I haven't got x-ray eyes, have I?"

"It's probably Sylvia," said Mum.

Over in the corner Granddad smiled.

"You see," said Grandma. "It's probably Sylvia."

John Watson heaved himself off the settee and went grumbling into the hallway.

Sylvia was tarted up as usual. She was still single and was forever in search of the elusive Mr Perfect with whom she could spend the rest of her life. Unfortunately she was too stupid to realise that the perfect man didn't exist and she usually ended up dating men who would inevitably disappoint her.

Her hair was made up in a beehive and she had doused it with so much hairspray it caused everyone in the room to choke as she walked past them. She was dressed in a tight pencil skirt and an angora sweater that clung to her body like a second skin and made her abnormally large breasts stand out like torpedoes. Granddad told me once (out of my mother's earshot) that he could always tell when Sylvia was coming into a room because her tits came in ten seconds before she did.

She beamed happily as she entered the room. "Merry Christmas everyone!"

"Nah then, Sylv," said Grandma, looking Sylvia up and down with her usual disapproval. "Been out looking for Mr Wrong again, have you?"

"Eeh, there were no need for that, Edith," Granddad said. "Come and sit over here, Sylvia. I've saved a place for you."

"Mind when you're lighting up, Bill," Grandma said. "Sylvia's head might catch fire."

"Leave the girl alone, Edith," Granddad replied. Then he winked and patted the empty chair beside him.

Granddad enjoyed Sylvia's company immensely because, like the rest of the family he considered her to be a bit thick and he went to extraordinary lengths to prove his point, for no apparent reason except to amuse himself. Being well read, he had a distinct advantage over Sylvia. She regarded reading to be too challenging and found it difficult to concentrate on the articles in the *Radio Times*, let alone novels that contained big words she couldn't understand or even spell.

"Do you suppose George Orwell was a *true* visionary, or do you think *Nineteen Eighty-Four* was really a metaphor for the decline of Western civilisation in 1948?" Granddad asked of her, staring intently into her heavily mascara'd eyes.

Sylvia spluttered into the sherry glass she'd just been handed and her eyes began to glaze over.

"Well?" Granddad asked, impatiently.

"Da-ad, do you have to?" implored Mum.

"I only want her opinion," Granddad replied, smiling mischievously.

Despite her rather limited knowledge of English literature, Sylvia tried to summon as much dignity as she could muster in a futile attempt to answer Granddad's loaded question.

"George Orwell?" she replied timidly, acknowledging Granddad's vastly superior intellect. "I . . . don't really know his books, but . . . doesn't he write . . . children's stories?"

"That's right, luv," said Granddad. "As a matter of interest, how *do* you keep your hair up like that?"

Sylvia gave him a bemused look that suggested she was still in a state of shock. "Umm . . . Hairspray," she said, vacantly.

"Fascinating," replied Granddad, who *was* truly fascinated by it.

As Granddad gazed in awe at Sylvia's gravity defying hair there was an unfamiliar knock at the front door followed by the sound of scampering feet and muffled voices from the porch. Realising the secret code hadn't been used, John Watson immediately sprang to his feet, switched off the television and turned out the lights. He placed a finger over his mouth and pursed his lips. "Shh," he whispered.

The room fell deathly quiet.

"*Si-ilent Night, Ho-oly Night* . . ." wafted through the letter box. "*All is calm, All is bright . . . Round y . . .*" the voices faltered momentarily "*happy, happy, happy, happy talk, talk about things we like to do—.*"

The singers outside were experienced campaigners and were now, with the grace and ease of seasoned entertainers, moving into selections from the musicals of Rodgers and Hammerstein.

"*Doe, a deer a female deer, ray, a drop of golden sun—*"

John Watson eased off his shoes, left the room and made his way to the kitchen, where he took a large butcher's knife from the cutlery drawer. He got down on his hands and knees and crawled down the length of the hall.

"*Me, a name I call myself, far, a long long way to run—*"

The doorbell rang and he quietly lifted himself up, silently turning the latch with his free hand.

"*Oooooooooooooooooooooklahoma, where the wind comes sweepin' down the plai—*"

John Watson had never been a fan of Rodgers and Hammerstein at the best of times, but if there was one musical he absolutely detested it was *Oklahoma*. He threw open the front door and, standing under the eerie yellow light of the porch, brandishing the butcher's knife over his head, roared his fury at the six spotty-faced teenagers who were stood before him.

"*GOO ON! GERAAART OF IT!!!!*"

The only thing the carol singers saw (in the split-second they were frozen in fear) was a crazed, psychotic lunatic brandishing a butcher's knife at them. It only took one of them to panic and flee to make the others follow suit.

John Watson slammed the door shut and made his way back to the front room. He switched on the lights and turned on the television.

As he plonked himself down into the soft warmth of the settee he turned to Grandma and said, "Aye, and a Merry bloody Christmas to you too!"

Big-Boned Girls
& Oxo Cubes

I grew up living with the kind of physiology that could devour any amount of food without putting on one ounce of weight. I loved watching big-boned women (as my mother used to call them) slavering as I tucked into mountainous piles of mashed potatoes and slabs of steak the size of my head, knowing that just a morsel of what I was eating would put pounds onto their hips.

My mother used to try and set me up with the daughters of her friends and as soon as she told me they were big-boned I knew exactly what she meant.

"She's just big-boned, Stephen," she would say.

"You mean fat, don't you mum."

"No . . . well, it's just puppy fat; she'll grow out of it."

"But won't her bones be too big for her then?"

"You cheeky bugger; you never listen to what I tell you. She's a right nice girl, she is; too bloody good for you, that's for sure. I don't know why I bother."

My mother was a reluctant cook and so it was odd that she agreed to let Uncle Chas move into the spare room and cook for him. My mother had told him that he could only stay there if he had a job and could pay his rent on time.

Uncle Chas was still trying to find his way as a jobbing actor and was therefore almost constantly out of work. He became involved with the Fylde Players, a local amateur dramatic group, shortly after leaving the British Army and, to his surprise he found that he was actually quite good at it.

He'd wandered into their rehearsals because he'd heard they had a bar that stayed open after the pubs chucked out. He was mistaken but, as luck would have it, the actor who was supposed to be playing the lead had suddenly been taken ill and after much pleading by the director Chas reluctantly agreed to stand in until a replacement could be found. A replacement was never found, but by the time the play opened Chas had already been bitten by the acting bug and was displaying a skill in characterisation that the other members of the group had rarely seen.

After his triumphant debut on the amateur stage Chas landed himself the key role in all the productions that followed, receiving flattering reviews in the local newspaper. Unfortunately these reviews only served to inflate his growing ego and he soon became convinced that he was a better actor than he actually was. He was revered for his acting abilities by the other prima donnas in the group and despised by the remaining members for his arrogance. In the wonderful world of amateur theatre a poor actor was good and a mediocre actor was brilliant.

He left the group to pursue a misguided career on the professional stage, but after two largely unsuccessful years in rep the work all but dried up for him and his inevitable decline began. The fame and fortune he so desperately sought quietly and cruelly passed him by.

By this time he was married and lived with his wife in a council house in South Shore. Like his acting career, his marriage was failing. When they had married he'd been full of himself with a promising future ahead of him, but two years down the line his wife was finding it difficult to cope with the peaks and troughs of the acting profession.

Towards the end of their marriage an apocryphal tale began to circulate around his family and friends.

It went something like this—

On the morning of his wife's thirty-fifth birthday Chas decided to surprise her by making her a cup of tea and taking it upstairs so she could drink it in bed. All went well at first. He boiled the kettle, put the required amount of tea into the pot then filled the kettle with boiling water.

Unfortunately this is where he ran into a problem. To solve this he went to the bottom of the stairs and called up to his wife, "How many sugars do you take, luv?"

"Two," came the reply.

There followed a few moments of uncomfortable silence before he called back to his wife, "How many sugars do I take?"

A few weeks later, after returning from yet another gruellingly unsuccessful audition, Chas came home to find that his wife had left him, taking with her the entire contents of the house. And if that wasn't traumatic enough, to add insult to injury, she had left him a four-page letter containing a detailed list of all his sexual shortcomings. This, coupled with his inability to secure himself even a half-decent walk-on role, led him to believe that his entire life had been a complete and unmitigated failure.

Shortly after moving in with us, he told the barmaid in the Halfway House that he just couldn't understand why he hadn't been able to land himself a leading role in any of the West End farces that were playing at the moment, because he, of all people, knew what farces were all about.

He had, after all, been living in one for most of his life.

Uncle Chas was working as a drayman when he was living with us and as a result he would spend long hours lugging heavy barrels of beer down into the cellars of the pubs in Blackpool and he would return home tired and hungry. He paid food and board to my mother regularly and on time and therefore expected to be fed when he arrived home from a hard day's toil. I remember him coming home one time and as he walked through the door his sister shouted, "Your tea's in't kitchen. You just need to warm it up."

At this point I should offer some form of explanation as to the meaning of what my mother said in the preceding paragraph:

If you are from the South of England you may, at some point in your life, decide to make the perilous journey north and visit Lancashire, Yorkshire or Cumbria. Once you have left the safe and insular world of the south there is a possibility that you may look upon Northerners with a certain degree of suspicion; if you do feel this way don't worry—it's a perfectly natural reaction and it does take some time to accept the fact that people you don't know can be helpful and friendly towards you for no apparent reason. But apart from the odd gang of clog-wearing youths roaming the streets with woad-painted faces whilst playing the theme tune from the *Hovis* advert on brass instruments, our only *real* difference is that in the North we have dinner at lunch time and tea at dinner time.

I thought what my mother had said was strange as I had not seen her enter the kitchen at all that day and, indeed, when Uncle Chas stepped into that rarely used room his olfactory senses were not greeted by the aroma of freshly cooked food.

All the really good food I remember as a youngster was cooked by my grandma; cottage pies, Lancashire hot-pots and (my favourite) ham shank cooked in a thick pea soup. I always had two choices for every meal—take it or leave it—and if I left it, my grandma would cover it in foil and it would sit in the refrigerator until the next morning, when it would be served up cold for my breakfast. I soon learned that if I wanted to avoid congealed food for breakfast then I had to eat *everything* on my plate the night before. After Mum married and moved in with John Watson the only food on offer came from either a packet or a tin and the only square meal I got was on a Saturday when I went to visit my grandparents.

"Where is it, Mary?" Chas called from the kitchen, "I can't find it."

"It's right next t'cooker," my mother called back. "You can't miss it."

Uncle Chas looked next to the cooker and there it was—a tea fit for a king. It stood proudly on its own as if to say 'Look at me—I am the cornerstone of any nutritional diet'. It was a *Batchelor's Pot Noodle*, and propped up next to it, placed there by my mother's own fair hand, was a fork.

When there were no *Pot Noodles* left my mother's idea of a square meal was an OXO cube.

Fun With Offal

Granddad always had a spring in his step whenever he took me off to ask Mr Johnson for some chicken's feet and sheep's eyes. Mr Gordon Johnson, our local butcher, used to tell stories about him and his wife's nocturnal sexual activities as he was serving his customers. He was a big, powerful man who wore a black-and-white striped apron that was usually covered in blood and the remains of some unfortunate animal's entrails, and if that wasn't intimidating enough he was never seen without his extremely large chopper in his right hand. The old ladies of the surrounding neighbourhood would queue up in his shop, but they were not there for his meat—they were there to listen and giggle to each other as he related his tales of late night sex.

"So you see, Bill," he said to Granddad as he wrapped up the sheep's eyes, "I had her on her knees and she was holding onto the bedhead for dear life, because you know what I'm like when I get going, and so . . ."

"For God's sake, Gordon," interrupted Granddad, "I've got my grandson here with me."

"Oh, right, sorry Bill."

He finished wrapping the chicken's feet and we left the shop.

The chicken's feet provided us with hours of amusement and, with practice and patience I learned the mystic and little-known art of chicken-foot-manipulation. Acting on his advice, I took a chicken's foot into school and used my newly acquired skill to scratch at the neck of Maureen Millwater who sat at the desk in front of me. When Maureen felt the scaly talon scratch her neck she leapt out of her seat and cried out in alarm and revulsion. I got sent immediately to Master Bates, where I had to explain, in words containing no more than three syllables, the cause of my increasingly anti-social behaviour.

Sheep's eyes were reserved for rainy Saturday mornings and old ladies with umbrellas. The way it works is this:

You hold the sheep's eye in one hand (it doesn't matter which) and you walk behind an old lady. At a given signal you tap the back of her open umbrella and when she turns round you clasp your hand to your eye and start to scream loudly, dropping the concealed sheep's eye on to the pavement at the same time. The old lady starts to scream and you run away laughing diabolically.

On the days when we felt particularly cruel we went to the Promenade where we fed the seagulls with chunks of bread. The seagulls would eat greedily and soar gracefully up into the air, unaware that the bread, laced with generous helpings of bicarbonate of soda, was already expanding in their stomachs. After a short time they would lose height and explode in mid-air, showering the ground with their innards. Granddad considered this to be a particularly satisfying trick if performed during high season when the beaches were packed with tourists.

He was a teenage delinquent trapped in an old man's body and he took great delight in teaching me things that would have shocked my mother to the bone.

One time he showed me how to fire an air pistol he'd secretly bought me, which I was never *ever*, under any circumstances, to tell Mum or Grandma about. I had to cross my heart and hope to die in a cellar full of rats before he would even let me touch it.

The target he carefully selected for our afternoon shoot-out was a bird box that John Watson had spent many weeks constructing in the back garden. Grandma hated it. She was never proud of any of her son in law's achievements and was highly critical of everything he did.

"Did *you* make that?" she asked him on the day he revealed his masterpiece.

"Yes," he replied proudly.

"I thought so," Grandma sneered.

"What's that supposed to mean?"

"Nothing."

"What's wrong with it?"

"One light breeze and it'll be in pieces. Remind me to never stay in one of your bloody houses if you ever decide to become an architect."

John Watson looked hurt. "I can't do anything right for you, can I?

It's true that time flies when you're enjoying yourself. It seemed no time at all had passed before the bird box was riddled with pellet holes and John Watson was going mental at Granddad who was caught holding (as it were) the smoking gun.

"You silly old bugger!" he roared, as he snatched the air pistol from Granddad's hand. "What do you think you're playing at?"

"Target practice."

"Target Practice? Bloody target practice? Who do you think you are? An assassin! That's not a *target*! That's my bloody *bird box*!"

"So *that's* what it is," Granddad said, rubbing his chin and winking at me.

"You know *exactly* what it is."

"I'm sorry; I just thought it was a pile of old shite."

John Watson was taken aback. This was the sort of thing he would have expected from my Grandma. "Have you any idea how long it took me to build it?" he asked.

"No. Enlighten me."

"Well . . ." John Watson thought for a moment. "a . . . a long time—that's how long!"

"Really?" said Granddad. "It took you *that* long?"

John Watson just stood there, his face turning crimson, and for one moment I was sure he was going to shoot Granddad dead where he stood. But he didn't. Instead, he confiscated the air pistol and went back into the house, swearing loudly to himself.

Just before he went indoors he farted.

Granddad turned to me and gave me one of his wry smiles. "I knew he'd do that," he said.

CRABS & SCABS

So, you're off to stay in the Watson caravan next week, eh?" said Granddad with a smirk.

"Aye. I don't want to though."

Granddad laughed. "Heysham, eh. There's nowt in Heysham, lad. They prop dead people up in bus shelters just to make the place look busy." Then he went on to describe how it wasn't the worst place on earth, because it wasn't on earth at all. It was actually the forgotten eighth circle of Hell, nestled secretly and malevolently between the Desolate Wastelands of Eternal Pain and Morecambe.

"He says we're going there to get away from it all."

I always called my stepfather "he" in front of my grandfather. I never used his name. It was a secret pact we had between each other— we never mentioned the name of our enemy.

"No, lad, he's taking you there because it's cheap. I don't know about you, but I think his mum's a bit on the strange side. It must run in the blood."

"Uncle Chas said he was a wrong 'un."

"Aye, well he wasn't wrong there."

Mum shook me awake at about six o'clock the next morning and told me to get ready. John Watson had been ready for an hour and he was already in a bad mood.

When I got out to the car Mrs Watson was sat in the back seat, scowling.

Heysham is about 18 miles north as the crow flies and it took us about an hour to get there. On the way I asked if we'd get to see the Desolate Wastelands of Eternal Pain but Mrs Watson just told me to shut up and stop asking such stupid questions.

The caravan park was just outside Heysham and was perched on top of a line of white cliffs that ran haphazardly along the rocky shoreline. Apart from one or two shops we passed on the way there appeared to be nothing else there.

"What am I going to be doing here?" I asked.

Before anyone else could answer, Mrs Watson stepped in, "You're going to be very quiet," she snapped.

By the time we reached the dark blue, four-berth caravan the light rain that had followed us all the way there had turned into a heavy downpour and we had to dash from the car, ferrying the luggage between us. The caravan smelled of old socks, mould and decay. There was a tiny propane cooker at one end and a couple of sofas at the other that could be converted into beds.

When the rain stopped we went for a walk to Heysham Head. It was a ten-minute walk from the caravan. There were a few shops there and a pub. It started to rain again so John Watson dragged us all into the pub and ordered himself a pint of beer and a *Babycham* for mum.

"What do you want mum?" he asked his mother.

"A dry sherry. And make sure it's *Sandeman's*."

"How about you, lad?"

"He can have tap water and like it," said Mrs Watson before I could answer.

He bought me a Coca Cola and we sat inside the pub while the rain hammered down outside. My stepfather gulped his beer, mum quietly sipped her *Babycham* and Mrs Watson stared at her glass of *Cockburn's* sherry with scorn.

"Are you going to drink that?" asked mum.

"Maybe," she replied.

When the rain stopped we made our miserable way back to the caravan.

It rained all night but in the morning it was bright and sunny. I was given a bucket and spade and we made our way down to the beach via a treacherously steep and rocky path. The beach was more rock than sand. Mum sat uncomfortably reading *People's Friend* and looking bored while I went off to search for crabs.

There were hundreds of them hiding in the rock pools at the water's edge and I scooped them out, lifting them carefully by their armour-plated bodies, putting the big ones in the bucket and tossing the small ones back.

It passed the time.

Later that day when we were back up at the caravan I sat on the grass playing with the six crabs I'd liberated from the sea. They scampered about, their eyes retracting every time I moved my hand towards them. I counted them: *One, two, three, four, five—?* I stood up quickly, but too late to fend off the attack from the sixth, lying in ambush underneath the caravan. It lunged forward in a swift mechanical movement, its foreclaw clamping down hard on my big toe.

I let out a shrill scream of pain and my mother tumbled hurriedly out of the caravan, followed by John Watson and his mother. As they watched me hopping up and down with a large crab dangling from my big toe they started to roar with laughter.

"Look at the little Indian doing his war dance," Mrs Watson said.

"It hurts!"

John Watson pushed past his mother, took hold of the crab and pulled it off my toe in one single motion.

"Ow!"

The claw left a small wound on my toe and when I saw blood I fell to the ground.

Mum led me limping into the caravan where she washed the affected toe and put a sticking plaster over the wound.

"Stop being such a baby," Mrs Watson said spitefully.

The crabs were gone when I went back outside. I asked where they were and Mrs Watson told me that she'd chucked the lot over the cliffs.

"What for?"

"I felt like it," she said.

In the morning my toe was throbbing. I was horrified to discover a yellowy lumpy thing growing there that looked extremely unpleasant, like some strange alien fungus. My first reaction was to pick at it. I was a compulsive picker of scabs. Some mysterious force drew my fingers towards their dull, hard exteriors. Picking at this thing, however, was not a good idea at all.

A sharp jolt of pain shot up my foot.

"Bugger!"

I limped over to where my mother and John Watson were sleeping and woke them up. Mum took hold of my foot and blearily tried to look at it while I hopped around on one leg trying to maintain my balance.

"Keep still will you," she said, prodding at the thing with her fingernail.

Another stab of pain tore through my foot.

"Did that hurt?"

I felt like saying, *Of course it hurt, you stupid bloody woman*!

But I didn't.

I just said, "Yes."

"Good," I heard Mrs Watson whisper from under the folds of the bed across from me.

Mum gave it another prod just to make sure.

"We'd better get you to the foot doctor, young man," she said.

The chiropodist's surgery in Morecambe was dim and gloomy, largely because all the furniture was made exclusively out of dark wood. The chair was made of dark metal with a dark brown seat. It resembled some ancient medieval torture instrument.

"Right then, let's have a look, shall we," the chiropodist whistled through the gap in his front teeth. He peered over the top of his bi-focals and made a couple of *Hmmmm* sounds before reaching for his instrument tray.

"This won't hurt," he said, wielding a scalpel in his right hand.

Funnily enough, it didn't—not much. I felt quite pleased with myself until I looked down and saw blood.

My blood.

My eyes started to flicker and I began to fall into a massive hole that had suddenly appeared beneath my feet.

"Are you alright, sonny?" a voice whistled.

"Nnneerr," I said, blearily, before I realised I was on solid ground, or at least on the chiropodist's chair.

"You fainted there for a moment," the chiropodist said.

Mum looked concerned as the chiropodist dressed my toe and as we walked out into bright sunlight she said, "I think I'd better get your dad to take you home and your Grandma and Granddad can look after you until we get back."

"He's not my dad," I said.

And then I limped to the car.

The limp was purely for effect. If my mother could talk John Watson into taking me home it may well turn out to be a good day after all.

THE ELASTICATED
WAISTBAND OF MY
UNDERPANTS

I was in Topping Street with Pete Webster and William Beck stealing comics from the newsagents. We stole all our comics from there, it was far enough away from our own homes for us not be recognised by anyone. It was my turn to steal the comics that day whilst Pete and William supplied the diversionary tactics.

We walked into the shop and as Pete and William occupied the shopkeeper I edged my way over to the comic stand. I kept a lookout from the corner of my eye, then reached out, grabbed a handful of *Batman* and *Spiderman* comics and stuffed them inside my jacket. I turned around slowly and started the long walk to the shop door.

"*Oy, you,*" I heard the shopkeeper roaring behind me, "*put those bloody things back!*"

The shopkeeper raced from behind the counter, whilst Pete and William frantically stuffed their pockets with as many sweets as they could lay their hands on.

I didn't know where my friends had got to in my desire to escape the shopkeeper's clutches. For all I knew they were probably still in the shop looking angelic, their mouths full of unmelted butter.

I ran as fast as my legs could carry me but the shopkeeper caught me by the scruff of the collar only a few feet from the shop.

"Gotcha, you little sod!" he growled. "Now then, what's your name and address?"

At this point I could have given him any name and address I felt like, the name of any one of my friends, a false name, Prince Charles of Buckingham Palace—anything.

Instead, in my panic, I foolishly divulged all the information he required.

"All right then, there'll be a policeman round to see your parents later. Now bugger off!"

The shopkeeper snatched the comics from me and released me from his grip, clipping me round the ear as I dashed off.

I stopped running ten minutes later and sat down on a grass verge under a Railway bridge. My heart was pumping ten times to the dozen; sweat was trickling down my back and soaking into the elasticated waistband of my underpants. I was held in a grip of fear so tight my whole body was shaking and my stomach felt like it was twisted and held together with barbed wire. It wasn't being caught stealing that put the fear of God in me, but the thought of what John Watson would do to me when the police called round to inform him of my criminal activities.

I needn't have worried. Things at home had gone way beyond worrying about my petty crimes. Mum was sat in the lounge nursing a black eye. I had told her about this, had been warning her since I was eleven. He had only started hitting her at the start of the year but as the months wore on his violent outbursts had become more frequent. Usually he hit her about the arms, but this time there was no hiding it; he had punched her right between the eyes. Her left eyebrow was blue and black and had swelled so much that it forced her eye closed.

But mum was a fighter. I knew there was only so much that she would take from him and looking at the anger on her face it seemed that she had already reached the point of no return.

I hated my stepfather; I hated living under the same roof as him. He was not the brightest of men and when words failed him he quickly resorted to violence. Earlier in the year he accused me of stealing a ten shilling note from his wallet. Rather than carry out an investigation to determine whether he himself had spent it or lost it or given it away he instead kicked the door of my bedroom open and began punching me in the chest, saying, "Where is it you fucking little thief, where is it?" My mother was downstairs in the kitchen when she heard the commotion and she immediately rushed up to my room to try and stop him.

"How do you know it's him?" she yelled in his face. "You're always losing money. It could be any-bloody-where!"

He was always losing money because I was always stealing it from him; a little bit here and a little bit there—the odd half-crown or ten shilling note that I thought he wouldn't miss. I had even stolen the ten shilling note that he had rightly accused me of stealing, but that didn't excuse his behaviour towards me that day and the violence he arbitrarily doled out to me and my mother in order to vent off the frustration and anger caused by his limited vocabulary.

"Where is he now?" I asked.

"He's in the shed looking for something."

Oh God, I thought, if he finds my hidden stash of cigarettes in the shed he'll kill me.

"Looking for what?"

"I don't know," she said as she stood up and walked into the kitchen, "but I've locked the back door."

When he at last emerged from the shed I realised that my hidden stash of cigarettes were the least of our problems. He had found what he was looking for and it wasn't anything like a packet of cigarettes. As he approached the house I saw that in his right hand he was carrying an axe.

He stood outside the back door and as he took hold of the handle and tried to enter he peered through its half frame of glass and waved the axe threateningly over his head. "Let me in, you bitch," he roared, "and I'll chop your fucking head off!"

Mum stared through the glass and began to cackle at him. To this day I still don't know why she did it; maybe she had noticed the blatant grammatical error in his last sentence. "*Or* I'll chop your fucking head off, you ignorant illiterate pig, not *and* I'll chop your fucking head off," I imagined her screaming at him.

But she didn't say a word—she just stood there staring at him and he stood staring back. He could easily have smashed the glass of the window with the axe and then chopped us both up into little pieces, but he didn't. Instead they just stared and stared at each other until he dropped the axe onto the ground and wandered off into the approaching evening.

"I don't know why he just didn't let himself in with his key," my mother said as he disappeared around the corner.

He returned later that night, drunk and apologetic. I could hear him in their bedroom spinning his web of lies to my mother, about how he was really sorry and how he would make sure that it never happened again.

"Go to sleep." I heard my mother say to him, "we'll talk about it in the morning."

But she had no intention of talking about *anything* in the morning.

It was about an hour later that I heard the first dull thud.

Two more followed in quick succession punctuated by my mother's screams of "You bastard! You bastard!"

The door to their bedroom burst open and I heard him cry out, "You bloody mad bitch! Look what you've done!" My door was open and in the glow of the landing light I saw him stood outside, blood pouring down his face from an open wound on the top of his head where my mother had hit him three times with a *Matteus Rosé* bottle that had been converted into a bedside lamp, but which now served as an equally useful bludgeoning tool.

He hovered outside my door for a moment or two and I could see in his eyes that he was imploring me to help him. I started to get out of bed but before I could even put a foot on the carpet I saw a flash of nightie leap up into the air, bringing the *Matteus Rosé* bottle down onto his head once more.

She must have thought he was planning to take whatever revenge he had in mind out on me and in order to prevent this incorrect assumption she acted like a lioness protecting her cub. Blood sprayed into the air as the bottle connected with his skull and he reeled around the landing for a few seconds before rushing downstairs and racing out into the night screaming, "Murder! Murder!"

No one was listening and before long the street outside fell into silence.

Mum waited for about five minutes before she went outside to check the street. He was nowhere to be seen. She came back into the house and locked the door. While she was out I went into their bedroom and saw that John Watson's side of the bed was soaked in blood.

I didn't hear her when she came back into the room—the fluffy slippers she always wore made footsteps inaudible—and so when she took hold of my arm I almost (to use an overused cliché) jumped out of my skin.

"It's alright," she said softly. "Come on and help me change the sheets."

Fortunately (for my mother's sake) John Watson was not dead. A Good Samaritan had spotted him as he wandered down the street in his blood-stained pajamas and had driven him to Victoria Hospital, where the top of his head was stitched back together again.

He was kept in overnight for observation and when the duty doctor asked him how he had so successfully split his head open he explained that he had been to a party and got so drunk that he had tripped on the doorstep and split his head open on the empty milk bottles that had been left out for the following morning.

"There's something I don't understand," said the duty doctor, "if you had just got back from a party then why, when you were admitted, were you dressed in your pajamas?"

To which John Watson unconvincingly replied, "It was a pajama party."

He stopped hitting us after he returned home from the hospital, but three months later he moved out, presumably to get a good night's sleep.

I never saw him again.

LUST IN THREE DIMENSIONS

Geraldine McLellan had long been the object of my adolescent sexual fantasies. She was pretty rather than beautiful, but she wore clinging tops and short skirts that accentuated her breasts and her lovely, long, shapely legs. When she walked her peach-shaped bottom moved with the rhythm of an exotic dancer and, if I thought hard enough, I could imagine the sounds of sleazy, sensual, late night jazz following in her perfume scented wake. With almost depressing regularity I would push my pen off my desk whenever she walked by so I could stoop down to pick it up, hoping for a tantalising glimpse of her stocking tops.

One night I dreamed about her stealing naked into my bedroom, her firm breasts bouncing to the rhythm of her long, shapely legs. Moving seductively towards me, she took hold of my bed covers and in one violent, passionate movement threw them to the ground, revealing my hardness and vulnerability. She tossed her head back, her long, dark hair gleaming under the cool light radiating from the lampshade suspended from the ceiling and screamed, "Get out of bed, you idle bugger! You'll be late for school again!"

And then I woke up in wet and sticky sheets to the sound of my mother calling me from downstairs. As I threw off the bed covers I breathed the forlorn sigh of a thousand wretched teenagers who were like me held prisoner by the unrequited love for my history teacher.

Pete Webster was waiting for me in the kitchen. Mum was asking him how he was and he was hopping nervously from one foot to the other. My mother was a small, petite woman with blonde hair and a ready smile. I grabbed a piece of buttered toast from a plate off the table, picked up my bag and said, "Right, then."

Pete smiled at my mother and then quickly followed me out of the door.

As we walked to school Pete said, "She's a bit of alright, she is."

"Who?"

"You're mum."

"Aw, come off it, Pete—she's *my mum.*"

"That doesn't stop her from being a bit of alright."

"Look, will you shut up and talk about something else."

"I was only saying."

It was history that morning and we could look forward to quietly breathing in Miss McLellan's wonderful smell as she walked by our desks to deposit the homework we had handed in at the start of the week. And after her lesson, with teenage hormones rampaging through our bodies, we talked about the things we would like to do to Miss McLellan and—more importantly—the things we would like Miss McLellan to do to *us.* She was a goddess to us and we loved her with all our feeble teenage hearts, and we held a torch for her right up until the devastating moment when we discovered that Miss McLellan was not Miss McLellan at all but *Mrs* McLellan.

That evening, in our depression, Pete and I had been rooting through one of the drawers of the sideboard in the front room of the house. I knew it was one of the secret places where John Watson used to hide cash that he didn't want mum to know about. I didn't find any money but what I *did* find there, however, was *a million times* more exciting than a whole wad of bank notes. Underneath a pile of papers and scrunched up chocolate bar wrappers was a well-thumbed, 64-page, dog-eared magazine *full* of naked women. Not only that—*it was in 3-D!*

Once I had the magazine in my hands Pete started to dig a little deeper into the drawer until he found a pair of the cardboard glasses with the red and green filters.

He immediately snatched the magazine from me and yelped, "Me first!"

We took turns passing the glasses to each other and staring at the fantastic feast of female fancies before us.

"They're all bald," said Pete, eventually.

"No, they're not."

"Yeah they are—look," said Pete, "they have no hair *down there.*"

Back then pubic hair was not allowed to be shown and it was the job of government appointed airbrush men to supervise the removal of any trace of bodily hair on the female form before publication. These tireless guardians of the moral high ground, however, were totally unaware that their acts of censorship were raising the temperatures of men around the nation who were now being turned on by the sight of grown women with shaved fannies.

Pete and I stared—transfixed—at those pictures for what seemed like hours; at one point I was so mesmerised by what I was seeing in front of me that I began to dribble down my shirt. We only stopped looking when we heard my mother outside the door. We hurriedly threw the magazine and glasses back into the drawer and pushed it shut just as my mother opened the door and peered inside.

"What are you two buggers up too?" she said. It wasn't a question; it was a statement, but I answered it anyway.

"Nothing," I said.

"Well make sure you carry on doing that," she said, before leaving the room.

The next morning Deborah Delaney waved at me from the other side of the assembly hall. Deborah was sixteen going on twenty-five and had already managed to obtain carnal knowledge of almost ninety percent of the fourth and fifth year boys at Highgrove. But Deborah didn't go out with just anyone. She only went out with boys who didn't ask her out. She had her principles. If you asked her out she'd refuse you; you had to wait your turn. Eventually when she felt you were old enough she would get around to you.

Deborah lived on the next street up from me and when I was younger Mum used to tease me about her, saying she was my girlfriend because we were always playing together. Deborah would sometimes boss me about when no-one was looking, but I liked her anyway, even though she was a girl.

Deborah was sat in between her two ugly friends, Violet Evans and Christine Smith and when I waved at her she whispered something to them. The girls looked over at me and started to giggle and I was sure she'd just told them about the time she tricked me into getting my penis out for her when we were playing in the back garden.

I was six at the time.

"Let's play mummies and daddies," Deborah said.

"Don't want to," I told her.

"I don't care if you don't want to, we're playing it anyway." She picked up one of her dolls and pretended it was a baby. "You're the daddy and I'm the mummy."

I sighed and said, "Alright then."

"I'm putting the baby to bed now, daddy."

"Where's my tea?"

"Make it yourself, you stupid bugger!"

I started to giggle behind my hand but Deborah shouted at me.

"Stop it!" I cried, putting my hands over my ears.

"We're supposed to shout at each other," she said. "That's what mummies and daddies do."

"Mine don't."

"That's because you haven't got a daddy."

"Have."

"Haven't."

"So?"

"You just have Uncles. They don't count."

"They do."

"Don't."

"Do."

Deborah looked at me and smiled. "Right, now we've had our argument we've got to go to bed and have sex."

"What's sex?"

"It's when the daddy takes his willy out and shows it to the mummy."

"I'm not showing you my willy."

"Go on," Deborah said, "I'll show you mine if you show me yours."

I thought about this for a few moments. "Alright," I said, finally.

"You first," said Deborah.

I unbuttoned the fly of my shorts and took my penis out. Deborah looked at it and smiled.

"Now you," I said.

"Nah nah," Deborah said, sticking her tongue out. "Girls don't have willies *stupid*."

I just stood there looking gormless with my fly undone and my penis hanging out when the back door flew open and Mum charged out. "What the bloody hell's all this racket about?" she barked.

Deborah's lip began to quiver. "S . . . Stephen took his willy out and he wanted me to touch it."

"You dirty little bugger," snapped Mum, slapping me across the back of my head with the flat of her hand. "You know what they do to little boys like you?"

"Ow! No, mum."

"They lock them up and throw away the key, that's what they do."

As Mum took hold of my ear and dragged me into the house I could see, through watery vision, Deborah smiling her sweet smile at me.

The next time Deborah treated me to that sweet smile of hers I was eighteen and she was working in the ladies clothing department of *Woolworth*. I've never been able to fully explain why I had wandered into *Woolworth* that day, least of all how I ended up in the ladies clothing department. It could have been nostalgia that drew me into its brightly lit aisles; it was, after all, the place where Pete and William and I had done most of our shoplifting when we were at school.

"What are you doing in this section," Deborah said, tapping me on the shoulder. "You a pervert or something?"

"What? No, I err was looking for something for my mum," I lied, realising where I was.

She smiled at me and then said, "I'm babysitting for some friends tomorrow night. Just wondered if you'd like to come along?"

My answer was a swift, simple, emphatic, "Yes."

The next evening I used some of the aftershave John Watson had left behind and splashed it all over, dressed myself in my very best, trendiest clothes and hurried forth, smelling like the cosmetic counter of the local *Timothy White's*, to meet with my destiny.

The couple we were babysitting for were already out when I arrived and they weren't going to be returning until the early hours of the morning. Deborah was wearing a revealing, tightly fitting top with a short denim skirt when she answered the door and I was hot and nervous even before I stepped over the threshold.

It was all very civilised at first. She got me a drink and we sat on the large couch watching telly. I had my arm around her and she had her head nuzzled up under my chin. When we started kissing I felt Deborah's hand move swiftly down to my crotch. I could feel my whole body trembling as she began to caress the bits of me that only I had ever touched.

"Do you want to put your fingers inside me?" she whispered in my ear.

It was a question that required no answer.

Did I want to?

Bloody right I did!

As I stroked the inside of her thigh, she moaned softly, spreading her legs at the same time, allowing my excited fingers to slide easily into the smooth cotton warmth of her panties.

A tingling sensation ran through my body as my fingers entered her, and the next thing I knew she had my trousers undone and my penis in her hand.

"Now, where have I seen this little fellow before," she said.

She did the whole thing in a swift and expert movement that suggested she had performed this manoeuvre many times before. This didn't bother me in the slightest. Like her, I was only there for one thing and everything else was of no significance. For all I cared the world could have exploded into a billion tiny fragments. It didn't matter, just as long as I got to shag Deborah Delaney before it happened.

She moved her body around and looked me straight in the eyes. Then she smiled and said, "I think you'll like this."

I'll bet she said that to all the virgins.

I wanted to say, *I love you Deborah*, but all that came out was a strangulated, "Nnnneeeeeeeerrrrraaaaaaahhhhhhhhh!"

Although my whole being was exploding with sexual fulfilment, deep down inside I knew that, like Pete and all the other boys before him, I was just a one-night stand, another sorry name crossed off an endless list. But, that night, as I lost my virginity to Deborah Delaney, all the carnal thoughts I'd ever had about Miss McLellan evaporated and for a few brief joyous moments I was the happiest person on the planet.

But, as everyone knows tragedy is never far behind joy.

And the biggest tragedy of all was waiting for me just around the corner.

Everybody Smoked
Back Then

Granddad looked different.

His face was drawn and pale, coloured only by the blood vessels that radiated violently out from the base of his nose, across his cheeks, like the disorderly threads spun by a drunken spider. His arms were laid on top of the counterpane, neat and straight, down the sides of his body. Hands marked with liver spots, dark and aggressive, betrayed his age. The most significant change, though, was in his eyes. The sparkle that was always such a dominant feature in them was gone, and in its place was emptiness, a void so vast that if he could have seen within himself he would have experienced infinity. He stared straight ahead, past us all, as if we were ghosts haunting the periphery of his vision. It was like he was staring through the drab, pastel coloured walls of the ward, past the town, the shops, the Tivoli cinema, where he had taken me to see *Batman*. He stared past the lush green fields that surrounded the town, past the fast running river Ribble, past everything he once knew so well, into unknown territory.

Laboured breathing, throaty, painful, guttural rattling was telling his brain what he already knew.

"It's funny," he told me in one of his more lucid moments during one of my many visits to see him in the hospital, "I didn't start smoking until I was in the army. Everybody smoked back then. You got more breaks if you smoked."

Grandma knew the end was near—she'd known it for some time. She'd been playing this moment in her mind for weeks, ever since he had been admitted into Victoria Hospital with the cancer. She felt a strange kind of anger towards him for putting her through this, for allowing this to happen to him. He'd been a big man, a strong man, scared of nothing and nobody.

He'd known that he had the cancer for some time, but it had only taken six short, painful weeks for him to waste away to a shell of his former self, requiring constant attention.

Granddad never really grew up. He always had that boisterous, mischievous playfulness about him that was infectious and corrupting at the same time. He put it down to his experiences in the war that he never told anyone about. He told us all that life was for living and we should just get out and enjoy ourselves. Grandma knew different. It was his *Irishness*, she used to say, that made him the way he was. It was why she loved him so much, *still* loved him and would *always* love him.

We sat at his bedside during those long hours of agonising silence. We didn't speak to each other. We passed the occasional forced smile every now and again, as if attempting to reassure ourselves that everything was going to be all right. But, of course we knew it wouldn't be. We knew it as much as he did. We knew that it would all end in tears.

Grandma saw his hand move—a tiny, almost imperceptible motion—unmistakable—a sign. He took hold of Grandma's hand and she understood the gesture immediately.

He was smiling.

"Edith," he said to her; an eerie lucidity sparkled in his eyes. It was like a veil had been mysteriously removed. "I'm sorry."

Grandma said, "So am I."

And then his eyes began to glaze over. Grandma squeezed his hand gently, warmly, *passionately.*

"I love you, Edith," he said in his last moment of clarity.

"I love you too, Bill."

The end came so suddenly that I didn't even get to say goodbye to him, to squeeze his hand and to tell him that I loved him one last time.

Mum put her arms around me and led me away from Granddad's bedside. I could feel her sobbing silent tears as she held me tighter. "He's gone, Stephen," was all she said, "he's gone."

A nurse told us what we already knew, that he'd passed on and that we could stay with him as long as we liked, but Grandma only stayed a few moments longer to stroke his forehead and give him one final kiss goodbye.

We left the hospital, stepping through the imposing dark wood doors into the rain lashed street. It was already starting to get light and the rising sun was casting a red hue on the wet flagstones beneath our feet. In the silence of the morning Grandma knew that nothing would ever be the same again and that her first Christmas without her husband since 1945 was just a few short breaths away.

She took hold of mine and Mum's hand and, in the growing light of day we walked to Corporation Street to catch the early morning bus home.

And as we waited at the bus stop the smell of last night's fireworks were still hanging in the air.

A Midwinter Night's Dream

It snowed heavily that Christmas.

Great flakes of snow the size of dinner plates spiralled down from the heavens, and by late afternoon on Christmas Eve, a thick carpet of brilliant white covered the ground.

When I was younger I would have been in a heightened state of excitement by now, asking Mum every half-hour if it was time to go to bed yet. This was the *only* day of the year I actually *wanted* to go to bed early. Ordinarily, Mum would have to badger me into it but, on Christmas Eve, with the imminent arrival of Father Christmas, I took no risks and wanted to be asleep as early as possible.

As the years passed my belief in him waned and eventually disappeared, to be replaced by teenage cynicism.

I turned my attention away from the falling snow and looked over at Grandma. She had moved in with us just before Christmas and was sitting in the armchair chain-smoking her coffin nails. Since Granddad passed away she'd increased her intake of nicotine and consequently the living room was almost always shrouded in a fog of cigarette smoke. She took Granddad's death well at first, happy in the knowledge that he'd gone to a better place. But, as Christmas drew nearer she thought of him more and more. It was if she was lost and was unable (or unwilling) to find her way home.

She couldn't even bring herself to be sarcastic to Sylvia when she called round.

That night, when I went to bed I sat listening to the clock ticking loudly on the dressing table between the plastic *Revell* models of Batman and Robin that I'd made when I was younger. For some reason I got an uncontrollable urge to look at my collection of comics so I reached under my bed and pulled out a large box, that was their home. They were all obsessively arranged in title and number order, with the exception of the ones that Granddad had brought home for me when I was seven. These were special, a reminder of him and his generosity.

And that night when I drifted off to sleep I dreamed like I had never dreamed before.

In the dream there was music in my head, some kind of buried memory that had sparked into life. And as I fell deeper into the dream I realised that the music was not in my head. It was outside. It was faint and faraway at first and I didn't register what instrument was playing.

But as it drew nearer I slowly began to recognise its unmistakable sound.

It was the sound of sleigh-bells.

It grew louder and louder until suddenly there was a thud on the roof, followed by a scraping sound, like something coming quickly to a halt. I could picture Mum and Grandma sitting up in their beds, their faces ashen with fear, thinking about the only thing that really scared them—burglars. But when I got out of bed and passed their respective rooms I could see that their mouths were open and they were breathing heavily, locked in a deep sleep that seemed unusual for them.

I left them both in their sleep as the dream took me softly down the stairs until I was outside the lounge door. It was slightly open and a bright warm light was wedging its way into the hallway. I pushed the door open and peered inside.

He was sat in the armchair by the fire, pouring himself a glass of whisky from the bottle Mum had left out for him. His face was ruddy, flushed red after being out in the cold night air. His beard was thick and white—whiter than the snow had been earlier in the day, and it flowed majestically over his bright red suit. His boots were black, the soles encrusted with snow and soot.

He looked at me and smiled. Then he raised his glass and said, "A Merry Christmas to you."

At first I didn't say anything, *couldn't* say anything. The words were stuck halfway between my stomach and throat.

"A Merry Christmas to you, too," I managed to reply, after a small, forced, cough.

After that, I relaxed and in the dream we talked for hours. We talked like we were old friends, like we'd known each other for years.

"One thing I've always wanted to know," I said, "is how come you can visit everyone in the whole world in one night?"

He laughed quietly and smiled at me through his beard. "Do you believe in me?"

"Yes," I said.

"Then your question is hardly necessary. I am where and who you want me to be. The magic is in *you*. One day you'll pass this magic onto your children, but for the moment *you*, and only you, hold the key to my existence. As long as you *believe* and hold that magic close to you then the possibilities are endless."

And then I understood everything.

He smiled at me again and reached his hand out, tracing his fingers down my cheek. "I have to go now," he said. "You go back to bed, there's a good lad."

And then he left the way he came.

Up the chimney.

He didn't climb up.

He just sort of disappeared into a fine red mist.

I stood looking at the fireplace for a few minutes until my gaze moved up and there on the wall above the mantelpiece was a portrait of a young soldier in a gilt edged frame.

I reached out and touched the glass protecting the portrait and said, "Goodbye, Granddad."

I sat down on the chair he had just vacated and picked up the glass he'd been drinking from. I took a sip of the amber liquid and felt the warmth of it run down my throat and a tidal wave of tiredness swept over me. For a brief moment I wasn't sure if I was still dreaming but when I woke up everything was dark. I could hear the loud ticking of my clock and I knew I was still in my bed.

The night outside my window was dark and the air was starting to freeze. Soon it would be light again and with it would arrive a brand new day.

I closed my eyes and, in those precious moments before sleep, I felt the law of universal gravitation working its invisible magic on me.

ENDLESS POSSIBILITIES

Above the fireplace in the front room of my house, secured in a new frame, the portrait of the young soldier holds pride of place. He is, as always, dressed in a uniform bearing the insignia of the Royal Warwickshire Regiment. His square face is youthful and fresh and it frames an angular nose, beneath which a disarming smile beams with optimism. He has thin eyebrows; they're barely visible, almost feminine and his eyes sparkle with mischief whenever you look at them. The portrait was painted by some unknown artist using pastel colours on white silk. Concealed beneath the silk is the original photograph, taken in 1915, two days before his sixteenth birthday and three days before his departure to France.

It's a moment, frozen in time. It was my Grandma's most treasured picture of him and wherever she lived it always hung above the mantelpiece.

Grandma passed away six months after Granddad. The doctor's said that her death was due to complications brought on after she caught pneumonia but I don't think there was anything complicated about it at all.

It was simple; she died of a broken heart.

I found Granddad's photograph and its silk companion in the *Quality Street* tin I had rescued from under my mother's bed. The gilt-edged frame had most probably fallen apart and rather than get it replaced, my mother must have collected the two portraits together and placed them in that tin of memories for safekeeping.

Maybe she thought they belonged with those photographs that were taken of me when I was a different person in a different time.

Who knows?

And who cares if the memories those photographs triggered were my own or ones that I have borrowed. They are so much a part of me that *they are* my memories.

They are what make me *me*.

I thought about maybe framing the photograph separately but after some careful consideration I decided to put it back where it belonged—hidden as it had been all for all those decades behind the silk painting of an unknown artist.

The white silk is now yellowing with age and the colours on his uniform have faded slightly, but his deep blue eyes have remained constant throughout the many years of the portrait's existence, and whenever I look at them I'm reminded of how much I miss him and I'm transported back to a time when I was a small boy.

A time when I could ride on his shoulders and he would never grow tired, never complain.

A time when he would greet me with a dirty old sweet and a hug that took all the air out of my lungs and he would rub his bristly chin against my soft cheek and make me giggle.

A time when I would hold my face next to his and whisper in his ear, "I love you, Granddad."

And as I look harder at the photograph I can imagine the smile on his face getting broader and I know that, wherever he is, he's happy, moving from one moment to the next with the woman he loves and has always loved and will love forever.

And, as I look harder still, my thoughts turn to my own children, upstairs in bed, their eyes shut tight in angelic sleep, locked in the land of their dreams.

What will they hear on this Christmas Eve?

Will they hear the approaching sound of sleigh-bells, the thud of a sledge on the roof?

Probably not.

But the possibilities are endless.

Endless.

Acknowledgements

Some portions of this book first appeared in a different form in my short story blog *Travels With My Rodent* and so first and foremost I'd like to thank my wife, Jackie, for encouraging me to begin writing that blog. Without her initial encouragement this book would certainly never have been started.

I would also like to thank my kiwi friends Jim and Claire Fryer and Aussie friends Tony and Asiah Vovers, who always made laugh and unwittingly gave me so many ideas for my next project.

Finally I would like to thank my friend and colleague, the marvellous Mr Andy Baker for giving up his own time to act as my proof reader and editor. Without his generosity I'm sure there would be tols of nistakes in this bok.

Lightning Source UK Ltd.
Milton Keynes UK
UKOW04f0649100315

247591UK00001B/110/P